Brothers

Brian Aldiss, OBE, is a fiction and science fiction writer, poet, playwright, critic, memoirist and artist. He was born in Norfolk in 1925. After leaving the army, Aldiss worked as a bookseller, which provided the setting for his first book, *The Brightfount Diaries* (1955). His first published science fiction work was the story 'Criminal Record', which appeared in *Science Fantasy* in 1954. Since then he has written nearly 100 books and over 300 short stories, many of which are being reissued as part of The Brian Aldiss Collection.

Several of Aldiss' books have been adapted for the cinema; his story 'Supertoys Last All Summer Long' was adapted and released as the film *AI* in 2001. Besides his own writing, Brian has edited numerous anthologies of science fiction and fantasy stories, as well as the magazine *SF Horizons*.

Aldiss is a vice-president of the international H. G. Wells Society and in 2000 was given the Damon Knight Memorial Grand Master Award by the Science Fiction Writers of America. Aldiss was awarded the OBE for services to literature in 2005. He now lives in Oxford, the city in which his bookselling career began in 1947.

of the Head

BRIAN ALDISS

Brothers of the Head

The Friday Project
An imprint of HarperCollins
77–85 Fulham Palace Road
Hammersmith, London W6 8JB

www.thefridayproject.co.uk
www.harpercollins.co.uk

First published in Great Britain in 1977 by Pierrot Publishing Ltd
This edition published by The Friday Project in 2012

ISBN: 978-0-00-748204-7

MIX
Paper from
responsible sources
FSC C007454

for darling Wendy
first to hear of
'The Bang-Bang'
rockin-anna-rollin
in the back of a Volvo
proceeding
like a bat out of Hell
from Hunstanton
'Well, I was shocked . . .'

Contents

Introduction

My wife and I were driving home with our children. We had been staying in a bungalow on the north coast of Norfolk. Whilst there, she and I had had one of those matrimonial rows that blow up now and again.

Suddenly, a dream I had had during the previous night returned to mind. 'A nightmare!' I exclaimed. Immediately, of course, my family wished to hear about it.

So I told them.

I had dreamt the story of two boys who were conjoined at the hip and could not be separated. But worse still, another head was growing from the shoulder of one of the twins: a silent alien head.

My daughter Wendy was particularly distressed – eventually I would dedicate the story to her.

The dream lingered. I believed it to be prodromic – foretelling illness – but I built on it all the same. An exploitive music company took up the conjoined twins; transforming them into a novelty number they called 'The Bang-Bang'. They performed with moderate success.

Looking up the reality of their deformity, I found there was a medical term for it: diprosopus tetrotus; a defect in human babies causing them to be born with two heads. Very sinister.

In *Brothers*, this extra head eventually speaks. After its years of imprisonment with the brothers, it has nothing good to say. It demands its freedom.

Yet it is a strangely poetic story, and the story of its publication is also. *Brothers of the Head* was the first book to be published by Pierrot Press. The Publisher there was new. He phoned me and asked me to meet him by a park bench in Red Lion Square. Was he a secret agent? An escaped prisoner? It was dusk when I went to meet him. He wanted me to write him a strange story.

The book was published early in 1977. It was originally accompanied by surreal sketches by Ian Pollock, which perfectly enhanced the story. Possibly five thousand copies were printed, two thousand of which were exported to America. The odd square shape of the book, the amazing illustrations, and my strange story helped the book to sell rapidly – so rapidly that the publisher (Philip – second name, alas, forgotten) flew out to New York to get his two thousand copies back.

They sold immediately, but nevertheless Philip went broke – such are the hazards of publishing.

Brian Aldiss
Oxford, 2012

Foreword by Roberta Howe

This volume is a memorial to the unhappy life of my brothers – their strange, unrealized, dual life. Although it ended in murder, and many people who like to pronounce on such things have said that my brothers' entire existence was a form of slow murder, they did enjoy happier times. It is not an easy matter for any of us to weigh up the balance of joy and sadness in another life, even one as close as my brothers' was to mine. Perhaps when we grow up we should not be so concerned with judging such things, but simply get on with the job.

When Tom and Barry were young lads, they did not realize that they were marked out from all other children. One thing was as strange to them as another, all was accepted without questioning. Father took us to live on L'Estrange Head when mother died, at which age I was only a tot of three and the boys mere babies. In the wild surroundings of the Head, we children were thoroughly at home. We all loved this beautiful spot in which I still remain. I'm thankful they returned to the Head in the end, before the last act of their tragedy was played out.

We could name all the plants growing on the Head, thanks to the teaching of our father. Down in the salt marshes, where the land is still regularly washed by the tides, grows a plant called the grass wrack. The wrack is often immersed in the sea for long periods. It can even flower under the water, and nature so provides for it that its pollen is water-borne. I often think of that humble plant in connection with my dead brothers. They also had their flowering, however submerged it might have been.

Nobody can deny that our family, the Howes, and the neighbours on the mainland, with few exceptions, looked on poor Tom and Barry as a stigma, a freak of nature. The boys, poor innocent mites, were never properly forgiven because mother – who was greatly liked by everyone – died in giving birth to them. At the height of the boys' fame, when they were universally popular, the feelings against them changed to feelings of pride. But there was never any real concern for their terrible situation and, when the end came, back came the old disgrace. Ever since, I have known ostracism, useless to deny it.

Laura Ashworth, who played a positive part in the life of Tom and Barry, would perhaps say that the only shame lay in feeling shame, in these enlightened days. But it must be remembered that we live in a remote and backward part of the country, and that the Howes had their origins here. Little has changed on the coast of which L'Estrange Head forms part. Indeed, there has been recession rather than progress, for my Aunt Hetty has told me how Deepdale Staithe was a fine harbour in her young day, until the channel silted up. It would be impossible for a grain boat to navigate now.

Of course, with my brothers' lives always beside me, as it were, I am still torn with emotion when I let myself dwell on it. I was unable to write their story myself, not only because of strong feelings but through my incapacity as an author; so I have put together what has been said by others concerned in the drama.

Going through the pages that result, I can only reflect that Tom could have become a happy man but for the last twist of ill fate. Most of his life was still before him. As for Barry – there was so much more to him than the anger and violence on which many people have dwelt. Barry hated his fate even more than Tom; yet hatred was not the only feature of his nature, by any means.

As for 'the other' . . . I'm long over my horror now, and think of it as one more grain ship that never sailed. 'The other's' channel to the sea was silted up even before it came into being. Pity seems to be more appropriate than fear or shame.

Here I wish to thank all who contributed to the narrative, with particular thanks to Laura Ashworth for her counsel and to Mr Henry Couling for financial aid. I thank Paul Day for permission to publish excerpts from his songs.

I also have to thank John James Loomis of the Canadian Broadcasting Authority for permission to include part of a taped interview made in connection with his TV biography, *Bang-Bang You're Deadly*.

1

Henry Couling's narrative

I am a partner in Beauchamp-Fielding Associates, a London firm of solicitors who have built up a particularly valuable connection with what is commonly called 'the pop world', which is to say the legal and managerial problems connected with the exploitation of cheap music and young people. My first encounter with the Howe twins, Barry and Tom, came as a result of this aforesaid valuable connection. I was acting on behalf of Bedderwick Walker Entertainments.

Since the Howe twins represented a somewhat special case, I had agreed to see them, and more particularly their father and legal guardian, in person. I took an Inter-City train from King's Cross to Lynn, where a car awaited to take me to Deepdale Staithe, a hamlet on the North Norfolk coast. It is a desolate part of the country. Civilization has scarcely obtained a foothold there, in all the centuries these islands have been occupied. No doubt a permanently active east wind has much to do with this state of affairs; only a moron would hesitate before fleeing to the nearest city.

The bleakest point along this stretch of coast is arguably L'Estrange Head, a natural feature lying between the summer resorts of Hunstanton and Sheringham. It is neither a true headland nor a true island. To determine its geographical status under law, one would have to decide whether its baffling system of marshes, creaks and rivulets link it with or divide it from the mainland.

There was not at that time, and I imagine there is still not, any way whereby one could drive a car on to L'Estrange Head. The lanes which strike out towards the marshes from the Deepdale Staithe-Deepdale Norton road, to wind across Deepdale Marsh and Overy Marshes, peter out in bog, or at embankments built long ago to guard against the floods which perpetually harass this unfortunate coastline. One can imagine that the entrenched attitudes of the locals is such that their initiative may run to dykes but never to roadways.

Be that as it may, one chilly April day I found myself stuck in Deepdale Staithe for half an hour, while my chauffeur persuaded a local man called Stebbings to take me by boat out to the Head, where the Howe family had its residence.

Stebbings was what might be termed a character. He was a young man, still in his teens, not unprepossessing, with a sandy sprout of beard and a habit of not quite looking you in the eye. He handled his boat and its snorting engine nonchalantly. Throughout the whole trip, he insisted on talking to me in the local dialect. I scarcely listened, so busy was I huddling in my coat and endeavouring to keep warm. The wind came in chill off the North Sea.

We took a winding channel which, according to Stebbings, was called 'The Run'. The tide was low and we progressed between mud banks for the first part of the way. So we got into the harbour and then through more open stretches of water. The view all round was desolate in the extreme. I could make out a couple of ruinous wind-mills standing above the expanses of reed and grass, then my eyes watered, and I resigned myself to wait. The motion of the boat made me queasy.

At last, Stebbings – who had obliged me by naming every sort of bird which flew over – brought us to the Head, to a beach which he called Cockle Bight. A short plank walk served as a jetty. He helped me ashore.

'I hear you be a-going to buy they twins off of old Howe,' he said.

'I suppose half of Deepdale Staithe knows my business, since there can be nothing else to talk about here.'

6

'A rotten bit of business it is, if you ask me.'

'I was not asking you, Mr Stebbings, thank you all the same.'

He said nothing to that, looking away from me. I asked him the way to the Howes' house and he pointed to a low blob in the distance. A slight apprehension passed over me; I made him renew his promise to return for me in two hours, before the incoming tide could prove too formidable an obstacle for his engine. He then swung his boat about and headed back to the Staithe with a cheery wave to me. I was left standing on my own.

The Head was a solitary place, built of shingle and sand, sparsely covered by vegetation, open to whatever weather the heavens chose to deliver. It was hard to imagine why anyone should wish to live here – but imagining was not my trade. Business brought me here; business would take me away again.

Cockle Bight was an extensive half-moon bay of sand which gave place to low grey dunes. I looked at the pebbles and stones beneath my feet. Every one of them carried, on their westward side, a tiny fan of sand, where a few grains had found protection from the prevailing wind. That same wind whined about my ears. On all sides were water and low land, the two elements divided by strips of sand or reed. The reed was always in motion. Deepdale Staithe was just visible across land and water. Stebbings' boat had already disappeared round a bend in the channel. To one side and ahead lay open water, the unwelcoming North Sea. I took one look at this wilderness and set off towards Howe's place, holding my coat lapels about my throat.

Hundreds of tern wheeled up from a concealed lagoon, sped seawards, and disappeared. L'Estrange is a bird sancuary, preserved by the National Trust. Albert Howe is its warden. I could find no blot on his record of service. His is a job for those who prefer a lonely life, or have reason to wish to shun other people.

Terns and gulls were the only signs of life. Then I climbed a line of dunes and saw two boys fighting some way off. Locked together, they stood in waving grass, their figures outlined against the waters of Deepdale Bay. They punched each other with concentration.

I paused. Isolation lent a supernatural quality to their violence. As I went forward again, the dark figures tumbled over and disappeared into a sea of grass.

Arriving on this bleak Head, one perceives only a flat and tumbled expanse of land, encroached on in most directions by the North Sea. However, a walk across it provides a different picture. I was following a faint track which led up and down through shallow depressions and low mounds; all about was a world of miniature valleys, narrow eminences, tiny cliffs and secret hollows. Dunes of yellow and grey sand, scantily covered in vegetation, marched towards the skyline. These features had been shaped more by the forces of wind and water than by the passive ground itself, as bone is shaped by pressure of tendon and blood.

In order to negotiate a dale, I had to jump a clayey creek and climb a bank. There were the lads, fighting in a hollow almost beneath my feet.

I had heard no sound from them. The constant noise of air, water and reed accounted for that.

Startled, I looked down at where they sprawled, fighting each other steadily with a machine-like hatred.

They might have been sixteen years of age. They were of similar build, stocky, with broad backs. They dressed similarly. They wore the nondescript blue jeans which were the prevailing fashion with young people of both sexes at that time, and woollen sweaters. Despite the chill of the day, they went barefoot.

The great difference between them lay in their faces. The boy who rolled with his back on the ground had fairish hair and a long face. His face was red with exertion; one eye had been partly closed by a blow, so that he appeared to leer up at me with what would be termed in court 'a malevolent expression'. His cheeks were stained by tears and dust, his hair was full of sand.

His brother had black hair which stood stiffly up from his skull. His face was round, even squat, his brows low, his mouth bright and flat against his cheeks. He also glared at me. I saw immediately that this dark boy had a deformity, a second head, growing from his left shoulder.

8

These were the Howe twins, Tom and Barry.

'Hello,' I said. 'I've come to collect you.'

They turned identical surly looks at me, nimbly leaping up. I thought for a moment they were going to attack as they faced me defiantly. Then they turned as one, still locked together, and went bounding off across the dunes.

It was clear to see then that they were one, inseparably joined in the middle, just as my client had stated.

I stood watching them go, clutching my throat, rattled by coming on them so suddenly. They were making for the huddle of low buildings Stebbings had indicated as their home, the best part of a kilometre distant.

There was nothing to do but follow after, keeping to the trail which now led through rabbit-clipped turf.

Nearing the buildings, I came to a piece of ground which someone had at some time attempted to bring in to cultivation. A few cabbage stumps formed the sum total of its crop. More poor tokens of rural living followed: an old broken boat lying upside down, abandoned lobster pots, a collapsed workshed, a fenced patch of ground which contained a flower-bed and some hens in a coop. Beyond stood the house and another building.

The house was built of stuccoed brick up to window level and lath and plaster above that. One side was painted with tar or bitumen and was propped by a large old beam. The general impression was ramshackle.

Afternoon sun made the windows bleary. It was a sick-looking house. Paint had long since peeled from porch, door and window-frames.

An oddity of the site was that the house had been built directly to the south of a stone ruin, so that all view of the sea was excluded from its chief windows. Presumably the builder had intended to protect the house from the more savage storms blowing in off the sea. Ordnance Survey maps label the ruin L'Estrange Abbey.

Almost as soon as I had tapped on the door of the house, it opened and a man's head appeared.

9

'Yes.'

I said, 'I am Henry Couling of Beauchamp-Fielding Associates. You are expecting me.'

'You'd better come in.' Neither his face nor his voice betrayed much more expression than his windowpanes. He never gave me his name, but it was apparent from the start that he was Albert Howe. Howe was in his early fifties, a spare man with a suggestion of strength about him. His complexion was brown and weathered, and brown was the colour of his sparse hair. His dress was a khaki shirt with a flapping leather jacket over it, stained cavalry twill trousers, and a pair of boots of vaguely military design. He stood aside to let me in.

It was not exactly a welcome, but I was glad to escape from the wind. The door opened straight into a parlour in which a fire of driftwood was burning. So cheering a sight was it that I immediately moved across to the hearth and stooped to warm my hands.

'Is it always as cold as this on L'Estrange Head?' I asked looking up at him. He remained – rather stupidly, I thought – by the door.

''Tisn't so bad today,' he said. 'We heard the cuckoo this morning, across them marshes.'

He jerked his head in indication of the direction of the marshes to which he referred.

His was a melancholy room. The ruin of the abbey cast permanent shadows into it. A light bulb burned overhead, picking out in sickly detail a profusion of birds and small animals which covered the walls. Rough shelving housed these stuffed mementoes of the living world outside; wherever one looked, dead eyes glinted. A well-loaded bookcase stood in one corner. Table and chairs and two old battered armchairs completed the furnishing. The room lacked, as they say, a woman's touch; despite the fire, it felt cold and damp, and smelt of old seaweed, as if high tide had been known to lap over the threshold of the door – a not unlikely assumption, I reflected.

A kitchen led off on one side, its door standing halfway open. A dog barked sporadically there, as if tied up and not hopeful of improving its position. I looked in that direction, to find two pairs of eyes observing me; two heads were immediately withdrawn.

As I rose, I saw that a loaf of bread and the leavings of a poor meal lay on the table, together with a dead seabird. The seabird was stretched out on a board with its pinions taped outspread and its gizzard slit open.

Howe came awkwardly back from the door and sat at the table, where he proceeded to finish a mess of bread, cheese and pickle on his plate. As if aware of a certain social boorishness in what he was doing, he glanced up at me and gave a jerk of his head, coupled with a quick funny expression and a wink, as if to say, 'This is the way I am.'

Drawing myself up, I said, 'I take it that you are Mr Albert Howe, sole surviving parent of the twins, Thomas and Barry Howe.'

'Tom and Barry, that's right. The twins. I expect you'd like a cup of tea. Robbie! Tea, gel!'

This last call was echoed by activity in the kitchen, and presently a girl came forth with a big brown teapot. Setting it down on the table, she poured a mug of tea and shyly proffered it to me.

She was a good-looking girl in a countrified way, with big hazel eyes and a complexion as brown as her father's. Her hair was plentiful, hanging down between her shoulder blades in an old-fashioned plait or pigtail. Like her brothers, she wore faded jeans and went barefoot, a slovenly habit, especially in women. Her figure was well developed; I judged her to be twenty years of age.

There was less unfriendliness in her gaze than in her father's. As I accepted the mug of tea and sat down, unbidden, at the table beside the impaled bird, she said, 'So you are the lawyer as has come to take my brothers away.'

I patted the briefcase I had brought with me. 'I am acting on behalf of Bedderwick Walker Entertainments, with whom I understand your father is keen to come to an agreement. I have a copy of the contract here, Mr Howe, and will be happy to familiarize you with its contents. We can go over it clause by clause, if you so desire, provided I am able to meet Stebbings and his boat at your jetty in approximately two hours' time.'

Howe crammed the last of his crust into his mouth, masticated for a while, and then said, 'It's for the best, Robbie, I keep a-telling you. The boys can't hang around here for ever and a day, not now's they're growed up.'

'That's correct,' I said, snapping open the briefcase. 'The contract guarantees you and your sons a substantial salary, payable monthly, for a period of three years. It gives Bedderwick Walker the option of renewal of contract for a further two years, at a fee subject to negotiation. Bearing in mind that Bedderwick Walker will invest a considerable amount of money in training and projecting your sons, the arrangements are eminently generous.'

'You're still taking my brothers away from home,' said the girl. 'Who will look after them, I'd like to know.'

Ignoring her, I spread the contract out before Howe, pushing aside the butter and a jar of pickle.

'I trust that your sons are ready to return to London with me?'

'They're willing enough to go, yes.'

He looked up with a helpless expression, and said to his daughter, 'Robbie, see as they're all packed, will you?'

As Howe picked up the contract to study it, I saw his hand was shaking. He had well-shaped hands, with long fingers. He watched Robbie as, without another word, she padded into the kitchen on her bare feet.

'It's hard to know what's best, Mr . . .' he said gazing at the dead bird as if addressing it. 'May and I got on so well, we helped each other with everything as came up. That's her in the photo over there.'

He pointed to a framed photograph of his dead wife, standing on the mantelpiece. A sepia face stared out at the world from under a large hat.

'I'm sure she would be happy with the contract as it stands.'

Still he wouldn't bring his attention back to the document.

'That May was a very fine woman,' he said. 'One of the best, that she was.'

I offered no comment.

12

'It wasn't my fault she died. Nor did I ought to really blame the lads for her death, because they couldn't help coming into the world the way they was. Though I feel bitter at times . . . Anyone would. I took up taxidermy when she went – got just about every bird as ever visits the Head pinned up here on my walls, Mister . . . Though I haven't got a roseate tern, which is uncommon scarce these days . . .'

He managed this speech with another comic face, giving me another wink and a jerk of the head as he changed the subject away from his dead wife, almost as if he were making fun of himself. The effect was somehow as sinister as it was ludicrous, and I directed his attention to the contract.

We went through the document carefully, Howe showing himself to be less foolish than his gauche social manner suggested. In my profession, I am accustomed to dealing with people who live solely for money. Albert Howe, I discerned, was indifferent to it; he wanted a fair future for his sons and believed he had secured one; the question of remuneration was a minor one to him. This factor alone set him apart from ninety per cent of the population.

As he signed the copies of the contract, the daughter appeared again, wearing a torn plastic apron over her jeans. She began to clear the table.

'The boys are ready, Dad,' she said. She sniffed as if she had been weeping.

'Come forth, lads, don't be shy!' called Howe, jerking his head.

The dog barked in the kitchen, and Tom and Barry came forth.

Contrary to my expectations, the twins were conveyed to London without difficulty. They loitered on the way to the jetty but raised no objection to climbing into Stebbings' boat when it arrived. They waved farewell to their sister in rather a perfunctory fashion.

As previously arranged, the car awaiting me at Deepdale Staithe conveyed us straight to London; I surmised that a rail journey might have its difficulties. Apart from visits to hospital and one appearance on a medical programme on BBC TV (the appearance which had inspired Zak Bedderwick to sign them up), the Howe twins had scarcely left L'Estrange Head, never mind Norfolk, until now. The journey passed without incident. They were interested in everything, especially when we entered the environs of London. It was dark when I deposited them at Zak Bedderwick's flat.

The car then drove me to my own apartment, where I was glad to take a sherry and a warm bath, and play myself Telemann sonatas.

Zak Bedderwick was every inch a business man. He was successful in the competitive world of pop music, and would have been equally successful in banking or oil. As such, he was in my opinion a rarity. Most of the big names in his field can grasp neither their own business nor rock-and-roll. At this time, there was nobody to rival his flair or the range of his activities.

He had appointed a manager by the name of Nick Sidney to concentrate on the Howe twins and lick them into promotable shape. The twins stayed in Zak's flat overnight and no longer. The next morning, Nick Sidney arrived promptly at ten o'clock and took them down to Humbleden. I doubt if Zak ever saw them personally after that occasion; like everyone else, he had a morbid curiosity to inspect Siamese twins at first hand; once that curiosity was satisfied, his interest was purely financial.

The rest of the story hardly involves me. Bedderwick Walker was not my only concern, and at this period I became increasingly involved with a lawsuit pending over the nefarious actions of a certain Foreign Affairs Minister of a certain African state.

In any case, little news filtered out of Humbleden. Humbleden had been designed for that end.

Humbleden was one of Zak's country places. It was a grand Georgian mansion (with part of an earlier Tudor manor still preserved) standing in two hundred acres of ground with its own private lake and airstrip and a view across the Solent. What went on there was nobody's business. All the same, rumours trickled out.

Nick Sidney's training methods were known to be rather rigorous.

He was a man in his late thirties, thick-set and running slightly to fat, with a shock of greasy curly hair. He had been a second division football team manager before becoming first a disc jockey and then part of Zak Bedderwick's entourage.

Sidney went to work immediately on the Howe twins. He got them cleaned up and groomed and suitably dressed, and christened them officially with their professional name, the Bang-Bang. Tom and Barry Bang-Bang.

Musical training commenced the day after they arrived at Humbleden. There were one or two second-string Bedderwick groups which Sidney could have used for backing. Instead, he chose a heavier group, the Noise, then being led by the guitarist and songwriter, Paul Day.

The Noise was in some disarray. Morale was low ever since its leader, Chris Dervish, committed suicide by driving his Charger Daytona into Datchet Reservoir immediately following a Noise concert in the Albert Hall. The Noise wanted a new image and a new direction; the Bang-Bang wanted a new noise. The two went together.

Nick Sidney had virtually built the Noise and their multimillion dollar success story, as well as Gibraltar before that, and he set to work with a will on licking his new team into shape. He had to begin at the beginning, by teaching the Howe twins to play a few basic chords on guitar and to project their singing voices. Fortunately, the twins – like every other youngster on the globe – were familiar with the conventions of pop. They disliked being prisoners of Humbleden; they had no objection to becoming prisoners of fame.

Their rages, their frequent outbreaks of recalcitrance, were dealt with by Nick Sidney with the zest he had shown towards Nottingham Albion. On the one end of the scale, he employed cold water hoses and a new-fangled electronic stun gun; on the other, he employed the more traditional lures where pop groups were concerned, the three Ds of the trade: drugs, drink and dollies.

Despite these inducements, progress was slow. I saw Zak on one occasion, just after he had returned from what he always termed 'the Manor'. Zak was quietly fuming at the lack of response from the Howe twins. I recommended sending for the sister, Robbie or Roberta, of whom the twins were obviously fond, to see if that improved matters, but Zak brushed the suggestion aside. He wanted the Bang-Bang to sink themselves into their new roles, not to be reminded of the old ones. A preliminary tour for the Bang-Bang, on a Northern circuit and with a tie-in with Scottish television, was already scheduled for a few months ahead. As far as Bedderwick Walker were concerned, the operation had to start earning back its investment as soon as possible – any refinements to the act could come later, etc., etc. Of course I had listened to similar talk many times before. Training hooligans to bellow and strum was nothing new in the music business. Nor was failing to do so necessarily an obstacle to a profitable career.

But the day came when my gogglephone gonged and Zak's face looked out at me, voicing a new complaint.

'Henry, hi. You know of a magazine called *Sense and Society*?'

'I do. One of the Humanistic Sanity group of magazines. Left wing, of course. Circulation not more than 25,000 a month. Influential among middle-of-road socialist circles, you might say. What of it?'

'I've just had an anonymous phone call. *Sense and Society* have time-tabled for future publication an article on the exploitation of teenagers by the middle-aged, treating them as another underprivileged minority. The article will instance pop groups and make particular mention of the use of freaks to attract live audiences, complete with details of cruel training methods, including use of electronic weapons. How do we stop them?'

'That shouldn't be difficult. Humanistic Sanity depend for their liquidity on voluntary contributions, including a substantial one from the Borghese Tobacco Corporation, who happen to be clients of ours. Will the information in this proposed article come within appreciable distance of being accurate?'

'That's what I'm afraid of. It's being written up by a woman.'

'I'm sure you can manage that better than I.'

'This isn't just a dolly, Henry. She's old. Thirty-five. You know her name. Laura Ashworth. Dervish's girlfriend. Daughter of the clergyman who was in the news a few years ago.'

'I recall.'

'She's a contributor to *Sense and Society* or whatever the damned thing's called. You know how she hates me, silly bitch. If she lets out some of the murkier details – particularly if she links the Bang-Bang's name with Chris Dervish – as well she might – then our goose is cooked just as our publicity machine gets into gear. Ashworth could do us a moderate amount of damage. I want you to get her off our necks.'

While he was making threatening noises, I was thinking. Laura Ashworth was an emotional woman. She thought reasonably clearly until her adrenalin started flowing. There were ways of getting it flowing again which could guarantee she never wrote her article.

'I don't see why we should have to trouble the Borghese Tobacco Corporation, Zak. You have trouble with the Howe twins and you have trouble with Ashworth. Why not put the two sides together and see if the problems don't iron themselves out? I suggest you entice Ashworth on to your payroll and despatch her forthwith to Humbleden. She will not be able to resist the chance of reliving some of her former glories.'

That was how it worked out. Ashworth accepted Zak's offer. Whatever her intentions were about discovering 'the truth' about Humbleden – which she knew from Chris Dervish's time – may never be revealed. A friend of mine wrote a letter to the editor of *Sense and Society* asking him if he knew that one of his female contributors had taken up employment with a right-wing organization with considerable interests in the Bedderwick Development Corporation, whose exploitation of black labour in Africa and Sri Lanka was well known. Miss Ashworth's connection with that journal was speedily terminated.

In Laura Ashworth's background lay an involved story which I have no intention of relating here. Suffice it to say that she was the only daughter of a Church of England clergyman who later abandoned the cloth, and that she had no real place in society. She was one of those drifters our age so characteristically throws up. Equally characteristically, she gravitated towards the pop world – one of those homes for drifters where the inmates have taken over the asylum.

At one time, Laura Ashworth had held a post in a Department of Abnormal Psychology in a northern polytechnic, after which she had qualified as a prison probationer attached to an open prison – another home for society's drifters. Whilst at the prison, she had encountered Chris Dervish, who was there serving a sentence for drug smuggling a considerable quantity of heroin from Bahrain.

It was at this stage of her life that Ashworth got herself divorced from her college professor husband, one Charlie Rickards, reverted to her maiden name, and devoted herself to Dervish. When Dervish emerged from prison – and of course his stretch in the nick merely enhanced the glamour of his image with his particular public – he reformed the Noise and went on two extravagantly successful tours of the States and Scandinavia. Ashworth went with him. As her enemies liked to point out, Ashworth was almost exactly twice Dervish's age. But she had stamina. She survived Los Angeles and Stockholm and all the godless cities in between, and lived to return with him to the relative peace of Humbleden when the tours were over. I was always mystified as to how she avoided finishing up in Datchet Reservoir with him.

Some claimed that Ashworth's influence on Dervish had a stabilizing effect, others that it was she who drove him to take his life. Nick Sidney informed me that she had a disruptive effect on the Noise as a group, by which I took him to mean merely that she was particular with whom she slept. Be all that as it may, and it is pointless to bring charges where evidence is incomplete, Dervish was a psychotic from the word go. For all his ranting before the microphones, in private he was an inadequate little wet. Which made Datchet Reservoir a not unsuitable terminus for his existence, whether or not Ashworth was involved.

How the members of the group would take to her reappearance, I had no means of judging. That was not my problem. The vital thing at this juncture was that she should not raise any adverse publicity concerning the Bang-Bang in the media, when Zak's plans were maturing. I let Zak get on with it and returned to my African lawsuit. He was running the freak-show, not I.

The tale of corruption in high places which I was investigating was not then public knowledge. A few newspapers had begun to leak circumspect stories dealing with one aspect or another of the scandal: some charges facing a British Cabinet Minister, the dismissal of the head of an international contracting firm, the disappearance of a well-known architect. The trial still lay some months ahead when I was flown out to the West African state of Kanzani on behalf of Beauchamp-Fielding Associates. I was able to question some Kanzani politicians. The Minister of Health himself drove me out secretly to the chief item of evidence in the case.

Fifty kilometres from the nearest river, two hundred and fifty kilometres from any township worthy of the name, we arrived at our destination in the bush. There stood a great disconsolate white building, its tiers of windows shuttered like closed eyes, its portico already in a state of collapse. This was the multimillion dollar hospital built merely to line the pockets of a few avaricious men. The main structure had been completed. Nearby, the foundations of an X-ray unit lay open to the sky. Goats wandered about the builders' rubble.

I walked through room after room, ward after ward, all deathly quiet. No healing would ever take place here. There was no way in which one penny of the investment could be retrieved. Only the termites would benefit.

When I flew back from Nairobi, it was to find that the Bang-Bang had taken off and their first single was already in the charts.

I walk left, I walk right,
I waste no sleeping on the night –
It's two by two, the light the dark
Just like animals in the Ark
Because I'll tell ya
Tell ya
I'm a Two-Way Romeo

Hatched right under that Gemini sign
Magic number Sixty-Nine
We're two in one and all in all
Shoot double-barrelled wherewithal . . .

Girls cumma my house, I let 'em in,
I say Wait, I say Begin –
At first it's strange but then it lives
They grow to love the alternatives
'N' then they'll tell ya
Tell ya

I'm a Two-Way Romeo
Bang-Bang
A Two-Way Thru-Way New-Way Romeo[1]

Looking back, one is astonished to recall the fury which accompanied the success of this execrable song. On their first Northern tour, the Howe twins appeared as support to another of Zak's groups. Their gig, as I understand the term to be, was closed down in Sunderland for reasons of indecency; with Zak's financial backing, the manager of the Sunderland club contested this decision in the courts, and the affair was given some publicity. From then on, a trail of accusations of indecency and innuendo followed like exhaust fumes in the wake of the Bang-Bang's speeding career.

A question was soon raised in the Houses of Parliament. National debate followed, to the strains of that tuneless song. Should the physiologically deprived make capital of their deprivation? Was it fair to themselves and their public?

We can see now why the Bang-Bang was difficult to take. At the time, much of the discussion centred on whether their songs and performances were good or bad; in fact, the question of art hardly entered into the matter. The question of morality was a good deal more pressing (but the British public is well accustomed to confusing art with morality).

Two overlapping areas of morality served to make the Bang-Bang hot news. The Bang-Bang were Siamese twins and therefore represented a deformity (for libel reasons, the word 'freak' was rarely used in public); should deformity be exploited in this way – indeed, *was* it being exploited?

And – this was the more painful area – should deformed people be allowed to flaunt their sexuality? The deformed, the handicapped, were supposed to keep quiet about their natural desires. There was enough material here to keep the pot of virtuous sentiment, seasoned with prurient interest, a-boiling for a long while.

Self-appointed guardians of the country's moral fibre claimed that sexuality and music were being debased, that national sensitivities would suffer. Then a Liberal Member of Parliament went on television to state that, in his humble opinion, it was all to the good that minorities such as Siamese twins should have their voice; and moreover that his family (although not he himself) had greatly enjoyed the energy of the Bang-Bang, as well as the pagan innocence of their songs. He considered them good-looking young men. He did not see anything unpleasant in deformity, and looked forward to the day when greater enlightenment brought multiple sclerosis olympics and similar events.

This speech was so widely reported, with further photographs of the Bang-Bang and other deformed people who had immediately sought to cash in on the Bang-Bang's success, that it drove out the news of two more African states, including Kanzani, being overtaken by Communist coups.

Debated, photographed, interviewed, booked solid, the Bang-Bang rose immediately from strength to strength.

Imitating their rough Norfolk accents became a national pastime among the young. Deformity became chic. Fake Siamese twins became the rage. Singing amputees appeared on the Palladium bill.

It was stardust from then on for the Howe twins: the usual vulgar story of success. Talk of wrecked hotel rooms, hysterical female fans, drink, and strong-arm bodyguards eager to do their stuff, only added to the excitement. The triumphal tours made in this country were transferred to the United States with even greater success, then to Europe, then to other parts of the globe. There was the special Concorde flight to Kuwait, the launching of Bang-Bang magazines, a raft of golden discs and, inevitably, the constant flow of money and more money, unstaunchable, like blood pouring down a drain.

Even in the grotesque annals of the rock industry, the Bang-Bang provided one of those fabulous stories which appeared too good to be true. Certainly it was too good to last. The celebrated film director, Saul Spielbaum, made a film with the Bang-Bang and Laura Ashworth (inevitably called *Two-Way Romeo*), with surrealist trappings; execrated by the critics, its takings exceeding such previous legends of the cinema as *Close Encounters*, the James Bond films, *Jaws* and *The Executioner's Beautiful Daughter*.

Into this story, as sticky with success as a treacle tart, the question of art scarcely seems to enter. The Bang-Bang sang no better and no worse than many other young ruffians who have made a fortune with a microphone, a glittering suit and a few rudimentary pelvic gestures. Their music was technically indistinguishable from other music of the period. But they were unique. They did appear to be 'two in one and all in all'.

Always behind the brouhaha pulsed a vein of morbid curiosity. It ran through the youngest fan as through the commentators and culture experts who used the example of the Bang-Bang to spice up their own theories. For the Bang-Bang was not a solo singer; nor was it a pop group; it was Siamese twins. And the twins' first and most perennial song – as Zak Bedderwick had calculated – provoked the ever-interesting question: what was their sex life like?

2

Laura Ashworth's report

Having suffered from years of snide innuendo, I will open my contribution to this book by declaring that my attitude towards Tom and Barry was non-exploitative. It started non-exploitative and it stayed that way. They were in an exploitative situation and everyone got all tangled up in it. So much fame just drives you out of your mind. The pressures are too great. After our first USA tour, Tom and Barry and I ran away one day, and we found a field full of big white daisies. We just rolled in them. The boys began a fight over something, but I stopped them. We were so happy that we started singing. I picked some daisies. Tom said he would buy me the whole field. Barry said he would buy it, he would pay more. They started betting how much they would pay for the field, how they would build a dome over it and have daisies grow there all year long. At first we were laughing.

Then they said how good it would be to convey the field everywhere on tour with us. They discussed how it could be done, how much money it would take. I suddenly felt the field was not real any more. It had turned into a status symbol, an item of cash flow, another cause of rancour between the brothers. I did not want the field and, even if I did, I would never see it again. Even if I saw it again, I could never be free in it again. I got up and walked back to our helicopter. They followed and we never said another word until we were far away.

Well, it is impossible to be free and very difficult to be happy. I had a trendy sociologist friend – had being the operative word, because fame loses you friends faster than failure – who wrote about us. He took the easy line that the Bang-Bang were victims of capitalist society. It was the sort of thing my father would have said. It was a fashionable, superficial, smarty-pants thing to say. The truth was that we were victims of society's pent-up secret wishes. The capitalist world has no monopoly on pent-up secret wishes. Everyone everywhere suffers from shortage of opportunity to fulfil their whole selves: it's just that *we're* allowed to grumble about the situation. That was what made Tom and Barry so madly attractive – they were like one person with double capacity.

Enough philosophy. Before I go into *us*, I will start with an outline of myself, the kind of girl I am, right or wrong, and what made me that way.

I was the only girl in a family with four brothers. They were all older than I. My mother died when I was in my teens. Funnily enough, I know I should miss her a great deal but somehow I hardly recall her. I do recall the vicarage where we lived, though. I suppose it was dark and awful, but I loved it. The rooms were like jungles. I was a little wild beast.

During mother's long illness, I grew closer to father, especially as my brothers left home. Father was vicar of a poor London parish south of the river. He was always working. He never relaxed. Something drove him. He was always 'kind' in a hasty way, rather as if my brothers and I were favoured members of the parish.

Mother was a hard worker too. Vicars' wives were chosen for work capacity, not virtuosity in bed or anything like that. She and father brought me up as rather a bluestocking. This sounds madly old-fashioned and eccentric but we had no television panel, and mother used to read aloud to me and my brothers. Once she read all of Winwood Reade's *The Martyrdom of Man*, which is quite an anti-religious book. And father sat in the corner, writing, writing, at his bureau, with his back to the light. He wrote gothic fantasies under the name of Nikola McLaren. Some of them are good. I re-read

Nightingale Summer recently and quite enjoyed it. In fact, I wept a bit because I thought that I as a little girl had served as the model for the girl in the book who is kidnapped by the gipsies.

My father's fantasies helped to pay for my further education. I can see I owe him a lot, but I wonder if he was not too negative to be called a good man. He believed in all the things that intelligent middle-class people believed in during the sixties. He believed in equality between the sexes (practically forcing me to join Women's Lib, which I loathed), in cutting government defence spending, in the abolition of all colour bars and racial discrimination (he almost coerced me into the arms of any black who wandered into the vicarage), better and more education for the poorer classes, unlimited assistance for all the scroungers of our society, vast aid programmes for the Third World, severing of diplomatic relations with South Africa (but not a word against the Soviet Union). And so on. From which you will gather that my father was also for the abolition of private cars, non-returnable bottles, beer cans, plastics of all sorts, meat-eating, tobacco, advertising, and almost all forms of alcohol, wine excepted – in short, almost anything that helps an ordinary citizen lead something less than a dog's life.

As you will readily understand, in politics my father was a watered-down Marxist. I only once saw him in a genuine rage, when someone called him 'a bloody left-wing intellectual'. He preferred to think of himself as 'practising liberalism with a small "l", as he once put it – 'not unlike our Lord himself'.

My father claimed to believe that the working classes had never had a chance – a chance for what he never went on to specify. He was also intensely patriotic, so much so that it influenced what taste he had in music. He once published a pamphlet on John Earle, a seventeenth-century bishop in whom he took an interest. The improving conversations which went along with our frugal vicarage meals in my childhood centred round the three Deadly E's, as I thought of them, Engels, Elgar and Earle.

Despite this dreary catalogue of virtues, I did love my father. I loved him in a sort of angry, admiring, pitying despair. He believed all that he believed in simply because that was what it was fashionable to believe. Or rather because that was what people in his class had believed a few years earlier. I can still blush with shame when I recall how he conducted a service one Sunday wearing jeans. Poor father! I used to argue savagely with him – simply because I hoped that he might by argument come to believe in his heart what he really only professed to believe. It seemed to me that in his heart there was no belief at all.

'You'll see how things are in the world when you are older, my dear. And that will be time enough,' he would say.

'Father, you are as sheltered from the world by your beliefs as I am.'

'My parish is to me a microcosm of the world. Its errors and aspirations are the world's.'

'You know nothing about your parish, nothing—'

'I can't let you say that, Laura,' my mother would interrupt. 'Your dear father has dedicated his life to the poor of this down-trodden stretch of London for over twenty years—'

'Oh, I know, mother, but you, neither of you see what you call the poor as they really are. It's all theory with you. Theory is everything to you. You don't give a bugger about the actual people.'

'Now, my dear child, you mustn't allow yourself to talk like that. You'll only regret it later.'

I felt even his patience with me was insincere; now, now, I'm much less sure of everything.

But it was true that he understood nothing about other people. Perhaps that was why he wrote fantasies (of which of course he was ashamed). He did live and work with 'the poor of the parish', but they knew how to protect themselves from this sort of cant. *I* knew those people. I played with them, I went into their homes.

Most of them didn't care a scrap for anything beyond their own families, their own cronies, their own selves, their own wage packet. They elbowed their way through life independent of all theories. I admired them for that – and hated them for it. I was working through psychology and psychoanalysis, those King Rat's palaces of theory.

Year after year, through my childhood and growing-up, father laboured in what he sometimes referred to as his vineyard, never understanding why he did not make contact with his flock.

He had sense enough to perceive that he had failed, that Ma Jones and Shamus O'Leary did not give a hoot about the plight of the workers in poor oppressed Panama or the starving multitudes in Bangladesh. What he could not understand was that he himself had never felt the bite of real Christianity. I was a Christian once, and it hurt too much. I gave it up. I saw my father was preaching hogwash. I hated him then.

The day came when something went wrong. Just one more small discouragement. He said that people did not look up to him any more. He went upstairs to see mother in her sick-bed. I stood downstairs in the hall and listened to him weeping on the other side of her closed door. I felt so ashamed, loitering among the plastic macs and anoraks. After lunch, which he missed, father came down pale and shaky and pushed his bicycle out of the porch. He cycled off to see his bishop and throw in his ministry.

Of course, he still had to stick around with theology because he knew nothing else. He got a staff job in a Midlands theological college. It meant the final break-up of our family, because the vicarage had to go (they demolished it and the next incumbent had a trendy flat above Hair Flair in the new shopping centre). I know father bitterly regretted all that, yet I did not care what he felt at the time. He was always so 'kind' to me, whatever that means. Kindness was another of his theories.

That was a desperate sort of period. Everything fell apart. While father was busy renouncing his ministry, mother died. I had been nursing her while working for my exams. I used to get up at six every morning, under the firm impression that everyone in vicarages always got up at six every morning. None of my brothers was much help – only one of them even lived in London.

The night that mother died, father was out, chairing a damned Save the Sick committee. I left her where she lay and went out into the street. I just felt ghastly, blank, sick.

A few metres down the street, I bumped into Ricky Hayes. Ricky was a young Jamaican, one of father's lost sheep. A bastard but with a great sense of fun – something as rare as the crown jewels in our household. I seized on him, begged him to buy me a drink – I never had any money – and then make love to me. So he did, so he did. Nobody exploited anybody, and everybody was happy. I desperately needed what he had got.

And instead of losing interest afterwards, Ricky, who had a lot of girls, kindly took me along to see Chris Dervish and the Noise. He knew the drummer. It was great, and not a bit like life at the vicarage. The din was intoxicating.

Dervish was not so well known then. Ricky took me backstage afterwards to say hello to Chris. Ricky was sexy but Dervish was just psychotic. He started to make demands of me then, right in front of the others. That also was not like life in the vicarage, but I didn't knock it on that account. Though I could see what a mixed-up guy Dervish was.

That story the papers kept repeating about my meeting Dervish when he was in prison was untrue. Reporters just crib off old press cuttings. Chris was so wild, so frightened under everything. He was longing for a nice quiet open prison like Parkhurst, where he landed up after his Middle East adventure.

I felt protective towards Chris, even when he was exploiting me for all he was worth. He was younger than me. I wept and wept when he drowned himself in the reservoir. I would probably have killed myself too, if it had not been for an old friend of mine at the clinic where I worked. (He was a man called Charlie Rickards, and I was never married to him, as some reporters claimed.)

Yet it wasn't really Chris who turned me on. The music did that. I just dug rock. The past ceased to exist for me, and the future, when Chris was up there playing. Maybe it was the amplification, or the sexual ranting, or the whole atmosphere of demented licence. I don't know what it was. I just know it wasn't one fucking bit like the vicarage. I was gone.

The whole ethos of pop is classless working-class. It's naïve and uncritical and inarticulate. Nobody knows what they are doing but sometimes they feel what they are doing. And sometimes they do it right. Way behind it lies black jazz and that too came from another sort of 'free jungle', as Dervish once described it. There's a feeling of native tribes, of ritualization – something much more powerful than words and music.

All that I felt – oh, yes, I felt it, and at first all I wanted to do was to hear the sounds and get laid. But my upbringing saw to it that a divided part of myself also enjoyed the feeling that I was rejecting good taste and the whole dreary Christian-Imperial tradition dying a death elsewhere in the country. No phoney 'kindness' here, just genuine raw feeling. Maybe much of it looked vile from outside, and it was often hard to take, but in its reality it seemed pure to me. At least at first. Some bad things happened to me at Humbleden in Dervish's day which it is better should remain buried.

Chris Dervish's suicide made me see life was not as simple as I had tried to pretend. Undisciplined feeling killed him. He could not cope with it. Many other people would have gone down in his position, adulated but a captive of that adulation.

That chapter of life was closed by the time I met Tom and Barry Howe. I drove myself down to Humbleden in my Mini. It was a lovely August afternoon. Although I was no foolish virgin, I did not know what I was getting into.

Humbledon I knew and loved. I liked its style. It stood for a self-assurance, a fine sense of established values, which you had to admire. The house was beautifully sited on a slight rise, with its lake, the work of Capability Brown, lying before it. Through the line of great cedars on the south side of the lake were glimpses of the sea, the vital sea where you could be a child again. Wave-sparkle flew into my eyes, blinking between moving cedar trunks as I drove up. Organic life moved too – swans, ducks, deer in the park, horses in a paddock, never ridden and restless in fly-tormented shade. What was it all but the fruit of 'privilege', that word my poor father could not pronounce without pursing his lips? I never subscribed to the notion that all men were equal, or not after the first time I went with Ricky. Besides, why did underprivilege build one half so handsome and enduring?

It was quiet inside the house that afternoon. Quiet, except for the sound of rock from a distant room. No one about. The guy that ran the place, Nick Sidney, was typically not to be found. Not that I felt any great rush to see him again.

In the kitchens, I found Tubby Puller, the Noise drummer, scoffing sandwiches. He greeted me without interest, as if he had seen me only the day before, and told me that 'the freaks' were up in their suite on the second floor. I climbed the stairs. Still emptiness. Loud grabby rock issued from what used to be the art gallery on the first floor. It pleased me that I could recognize Paul Day's guitar.

On the second floor, the house became meaner, the corridor narrower, the rooms smaller. This had been the servants' floor in the old days.

I walked along the corridor. Someone was playing an electric guitar badly. When I came to the appropriate door, I knocked and marched in.

I had done a fair amount of research on Tom and Barry for my article for *Sense and Society*, and knew what there was to know about them. I had not met them. My first impression was of confusion – and something else, not quite horror, not quite terror, almost awe.

They were too close. They were always a crowd. They grew together like two trees growing where only one should be, branches hopelessly intertwined, distorting each other.

That was my first impression – one of entanglement. So wild were they, that they leapt up as soon as I entered. I had only an impression of their previous attitude, with Barry sitting on the swelling curve of a Victorian sofa arm while Tom attempted to sprawl beside him. Barry was plucking a guitar while Tom tried to read a paperback book. Their elbows got in each other's way. The thought crossed my mind that both guitar playing and reading were so foredoomed to failure that they were glad of the diversion I caused.

But it was not like that. They were genuinely wild, backing away from me like untrusting dogs. They were joined to each other just below the shoulder and at the hip. On Barry's other shoulder was that other head, leaning forward in an attitude of sleep.

'What do you want?' Barry asked.

'I'm a new member of Zak's staff. Hello. The name's Laura Ashworth, and I could use a drink.'

'Pub's down the road,' said Tom. They stood on guard, weighing me up, and I countered with my own curious stare. You could not help staring. There was a compulsion to stare.

The twins were strapping young men of eighteen, not fourteen or fifteen as some accounts have claimed. Tension marked them. Barry was more sturdily built than his brother; he had a red peasant face, complete with snub nose and startling light grey eyes which generally regarded you through half-closed lids, as if he were tired, or dangerous, or forever summing you up. His thatch of thick black hair stood up spikily from his low forehead. Tom was not so thick-set and looked slightly taller, though he carried his head to one side. His face was less flushed and thinner than his brother's. The hair that curled attractively about his neck and ears was a nondescript brown. He appeared more vulnerable than his brother. While he offered me a tentative smile, his brother scowled. There was a sensuous expression about Tom's lips, I thought.

Looking back, I can no longer be sure of first impressions. I was full of a sort of terror. Though I immediately felt their differences, I was also conscious of their blanket similarity, caused by their inseparable state.

Yet that head dozing on Barry's shoulder set them apart. It made Barry the deformed twin, as well as the one with power. On that first meeting, I scarcely dared look at it. Afterwards, my glances were always covert – although the fact that it has lain on a pillow against my head makes me as familiar with it as the next person.

The third head seemed to have no relation to Tom or Barry. It lay in repose on Barry's left shoulder, nodding forward. Barry always held his head away from it, which caused Tom to carry his head straining slightly to the right, so that he always looked at you slightly awry. The third head was small. It appeared to belong to an old man; its features were withered, its hair grey. Its eyes were closed, the eye-sockets sunken. Later I saw how greatly it resembled Barry's face, despite its pallor, which contrasted with his ruddiness.

'I thought you'd offer me a drink,' I said.

'We're going out,' said Barry.

A struggle took place between them, though neither changed position. It was a battle of wills, of impulses, of hesitations, expressed in tensed muscles, clenched fists. Barry took a step forward.

'We're going *out*,' he said.

Then they were like liquid. The struggle was over, they ran forward with uncanny coordination, four legs complexly moving, as they passed me and headed for the door. In a moment they were gone. As they reached the stairs, they gave a strange united yell, a noise that might have been fear or derision or exultation.

I stood in their room, listening to the sounds of their descent through the house until it was drowned by the music. I was shaken. For a moment, I had thought they were going to attack me. But it was more than that. Their presence had been a challenge to my own being.

At last I turned. Before I reached the door, a movement through the windows caught my eye. The twins were out there.

I went over and looked down. Still running, they had crossed the drive to the paddock. Lightly, they vaulted together over the fence to where four hunters stood in the shade of spreading oaks. They formed one figure when they ran – that was when their unity was most sharply expressed. No two ordinary people could run that close.

The horses backed away. The twins did not pause. Grabbing a mane, they launched themselves up and were astride in no time. It looked from where I was as if each had a leg on either side of the animal's back. Before I could be sure, they had kicked the horse into action and were off, galloping madly away, parallel to the white fence, dashing through sun and shadow.

Having gone into much detail about my first encounter with the twins, and how that first encounter came about, I find myself in difficulty about proceeding. What happened between Tom and me, and between Barry and me, is private. It may sound funny for a journalist to say that, but I do think that the more details I fill in, the less the magic of what happened will be recaptured. Because I did come to love them both.

An outline it will have to be. A silhouette. The twins got to know me. I stayed unobtrusive, attending their music lessons and the afternoon sessions with the group, and talking to people they were talking to, like Paul Day, the Noise's guitarist, for whom I had always had respect. I chugged round the lake in Zak's launch with them, I went on the beach with them, I even rode a horse for their sake – though not bareback. Some of it was fun. More often, it was pain.

There was so much hatred. Nick Sidney treated the twins as freaks; he had a special weapon – a stun gun – to deal with them, as if he were a wild animal trainer. He had established a pecking order in the manor. The members of the Noise were accommodated as he was, in luxurious rooms on the first floor. When I was offered a similar room, I refused it and took an attic room in the servants' quarters, where the twins were exiled. They were supposed to eat alone.

Of course, they were rough country lads. But that was not the trouble. The trouble was that they hated Nick, they hated the Noise, they hated each other. They hated their distant father for 'selling them', as they put it.

But they enjoyed the singing. They liked to bellow and stamp and project themselves. They wished to be the Bang-Bang and to rant and caper before screaming audiences. This wish was so strong that they submitted to Nick Sidney, up to a point. Training sessions were alarming feats of antagonism, with the Noise rebellious, hating the Bang-Bang and trying to outplay them. In trying to hold it all in one piece, Sidney drank more than ever and used his fists when he felt like it.

The exception to all this antagonism was Paul Day, who rode along with it as if enjoying the storms. He had become a lot more together since the days of Dervish.

Even the sessions failed to unite Tom and Barry. They found it impossible to play guitar together. Their tensions destroyed their sense of unison. Fights broke out, instruments were destroyed. Tom was really not a fighter, although he fought his brother savagely in self-defence. Barry might have been wrestling with a devil. He fought Tom, he fought the Noise, he fought anyone who came within range, including Nick Sidney. Sidney fought back; Sidney used his stun gun.

After one hellish struggle, Barry hit Sidney behind the ear with the edge of an electric guitar and laid him out cold. The twins ran, and were later seen perched on the roof of Humbleden, crouching by a chimney-stack. When I stood in the courtyard and called to them to come down, Barry flung a tile at me.

Some days later, after another violent scene, I phoned Zak Bedderwick. We had never been on particularly good terms, but he was civil enough. I respected him more than he did me; surprisingly enough, he knew a fair bit about music. I asked him if he would summon a qualified surgeon to come and give the twins a thorough examination.

'I know what's on your mind,' he said. 'You'd better forget it. They can't be separated and that's final. Besides, if they were separated, we wouldn't have an act.'

'You may not have an act as it is. They are all set to destroy everything. Look, Zak, I know something about their sort of mentality, and they are in pain – mental pain, right? Get another medical opinion. Maybe you could offer them separation in five years if they cooperate now. That could be the only way. Otherwise, someone could get killed.'

'You really go for that kind of drama, Sunshine, don't you?'

But he gave in and sent a surgeon to Humbleden.

Zak may have suspected that I was in some way going to get him adverse publicity if a surgeon arrived, since a surgeon could be said to emphasize the medical oddity of Tom and Barry. Although I feared for the mental stability of the twins, I had already given up any idea of writing them up as objects of exploitation. I sensed in them, as

35

in Chris Dervish before them, a blind urge to be exploited. They wanted the world to know of them. I was not going to make theory fit reality, as my father would have done.

The surgeon was Sir Allardyce Stevens. He was a small dapper man in his late sixties, with pale translucent skin and light eyes. He looked as if you could blow him over, and his smile was the gentlest thing I had ever seen. I feared for him in the presence of the terrible twins, yet they became as docile as lambs as soon as they saw him. What they hoped for from him was, I suppose, obvious enough. Sir Allardyce was a man to inspire hope.

He was with the twins for more than two hours.

He talked to me afterwards. Much of what he said was technical and over my head, but the gist of it was clear. Tom and Barry were conjoined twins, joined by ligament from breastbone to hip, in the manner of the original Siamese twins. Their circulatory systems communicated and, as is apparently typical in trunk fusions, they shared organs, including kidneys and other minor bits and pieces I had never heard of.

I felt flattered by Sir Allardyce's careful explanation and his assumption that I cared. I took him for a drink before his chauffeur drove him back to London. He went into medical details about how surgery was still not advanced enough to separate the two of them and have them both live. There were reasonable guarantees that one would live but not both.

'Which one?' I asked.

'That would have to be decided, my dear,' he said, sipping his brandy and tonic and smiling at me. 'Speaking as a surgeon, I would prefer to see Tom survive. Theirs is an unusual case. Superficially, they are symmetrical twins, as were Chang and Eng, the original pair. But Barry himself forms a host or autosite member of a secondary twinning. That extraordinary head on his shoulder forms an undeveloped parasite. It represents a third twin, a triplet or the beginning of one, as you might say, and is dependent on Barry, its host, for nutrition.'

'A parasite! Is it alive? Couldn't you operate and remove it?'

He pursed his lips. 'I wouldn't care to be the one to try; there are too many random factors. At birth, it would have been a different matter. As for the question of *life* in the parasite, well, not only that . . .'

He hesitated.

'Go on.'

'Barry is not a communicative lad, as you know. But he said an odd thing to me. I questioned him about the head – for which he has a name, by the way. Significant, that. He wouldn't tell me the name, and I didn't press him. He feels protective about it. He said that he relies on the third head.'

'Relies on it? How?'

'He's just a simple Norfolk lad. His attitude is partly superstitious.'

'But is the head . . . alive?'

'Certainly it is alive, or otherwise decomposition would have set in long ago. A more pertinent question concerns cerebral activity. Apparently that question was not considered during previous examinations. The eyes are permanently closed, but I observed REM activity.'

'What's REM?'

'Rapid Eye Movement. Suggesting strongly that the third head is in a dreaming state.'

We were sitting in the bar on the ground floor, in what had once been the library. All books had long ago disappeared. There were some comics on one of the tables nearby. Sunshine poured through the stained glass and coloured crimson and green the carpet at our feet. There we sat, having this extraordinary conversation. I hardly knew what to say.

'A dreaming state . . . You mean – the third head could wake up at any time?'

Sir Allardyce took a long sip of his drink and gazed at me as he did so. He smiled. His reassuring manner was at variance with the alarming information he was giving me.

'We are entering rather a speculative area of discussion. I do not believe it likely that the third head will "wake up", since its brain has given no indication in eighteen years that it functions normally. As far as we can tell without more rigorous examination, it has remained and will remain in a state of permanent unconsciousness.'

'Nevertheless, it is . . . a person?'

'A latent personality, certainly, yes. But destined to remain latent, unless some unexpected shock wakens it to life.'

I wanted to ask him what would happen then, but the question was too fantastic. I remained silent, trying to digest the information he had given me.

'It must be a bit creepy for Barry, come to think of it, always having that head with its closed eyes so near to you, mustn't it?' I laughed uneasily.

The laugh sounded like a giggle to me. Sir Allardyce laughed heartily in return.

'Indeed, yes, a bit creepy.'

'Perhaps that's why Tom seems the more normal of the two. He's really a dear . . . And you'd have him survive – if it ever came to an operation?'

The brandy was doing him good. He crossed his neat legs and relaxed. 'As I have said, such an operation is quite out of the question at present, except in an emergency. Modern medicine can supply simple spare parts – like artificial hearts, which are really only straightforward pumps – but we still cannot manage the complicated biological engineering which would be required in a separation, were both twins to survive such an operation.'

We were sitting closely together. I suddenly perceived that he fancied me sexually. A familiar mingling of curiosity, defensiveness, pleasure and power came over me. He was a bit long in the tooth for that sort of thing. On the other hand, I could not help liking him very much, and admiring the qualities I sensed in his mind.

As if he appreciated the current of my feelings, he rose and bought us both another drink. We began to talk more generally.

When it was time for him to leave, he took my hand.

'Is there anything I can do for the twins?' I asked him.

He gave me a straight look which had in it both malice and humour. 'I don't know; is there?'

I looked down and saw how plump and brown my hand was between his. His were thin papery hands, marked with veins and liver spots. But there was still strength in them.

He said, 'You are beautiful, Laura, and I see formidable qualities in you. Don't get too emotionally involved with the Howes – though, heaven knows, they need someone like you. It could bring you a lot of unhappiness.'

Before I could think of an appropriate answer, he had climbed into his car. A wave of the hand and he was gone.

I went back into the bar, feeling I should have responded more adequately. I ordered another drink, then decided I had had enough.

Nick Sidney came into the bar, flushed in the face.

'There you are. Now that that bloody old queer's gone, perhaps you'll do the job you came down here to do and go and look after those bloody freaks. Didn't you hear the racket? They've been busting up the studio one more time.'

'You're an uncouth bastard, Nick,' I said, as I walked past him.

'And proud of it. How else would I survive with this shower?'

After this exchange, I proceeded upstairs. The twins had been doing a certain amount of damage, nothing serious. They were objecting again to the way they were being treated. This anger against others turned, as it frequently did, into a fight with themselves. Barry was particularly frightening in his anger fits. His face became distorted. Even the third head, the one for which he had a secret name, took on a different appearance. The cheeks of its face flushed. I wondered if I would have noticed that detail in the general rumpus, had it not been for the conversation with Sir Allardyce.

They had a method of dealing with Barry's anger. Zak Bedderwick had provided Sidney with a Japanese-made stun gun, as I mentioned. I never understood how it worked, except that it was electronic; when you fired it against someone's temples it switched the brain's Alpha rhythms to Delta rhythms, thus changing the wave frequency so that the victim fell into a deep sleep. This handy instrument was used to put Barry out when he was causing trouble.

This treatment became the rule throughout the whole success period of the Bang-Bang, especially on tour, when the stresses were particularly great. During the periods when Barry was unconscious I was able to talk to Tom. I grew very fond of him, despite Sir Allardyce's warning. I feared the situation and would not have had anything happen to Tom; but it was not that alone which drew me.

At the height of their success, after the Scandinavian tour, I was separated from the twins. I believe that I was a good influence on them, despite stories to the contrary. But some people, among them the lawyer, Henry Couling (a sort of self-appointed guardian to the twins, although he did nothing to help them), decided I was a cause for scandal in associating closely with both of the twins. Eventually Zak Bedderwick and Nick Sidney got rid of me. My feelings were bitter, although I knew how little personal feelings count in the pop industry.

In respect to certain aspects of this matter, on which no doubt others will offer distorted versions of the truth, I would like to say only that the drugs in the case have been exaggerated by the media. They were Sidney's idea in the first place. I came to use them reluctantly.

As for the immorality charges, understanding people will realize that Tom and Barry needed love and sex just like anyone else, and suffered from deprivation. There was a jealousy between them, as between all brothers, but, in view of their physical inseparability, it was inevitable that any woman who came close to either of them would have to make what accommodation she could to both.

I prefer not to be more explicit.

3

Excerpt from taped interview with Nickolas Sidney

Interviewed by John James Loomis of the Canadian Broadcasting Authority.

JOHN JAMES LOOMIS: Now if we might move to a more controversial area, Nick, concerning the part Laura Ashworth played in the Bang-Bang's affairs.

NICKOLAS SIDNEY: No, there was nothing controversial. You know what it is, you're running a group, you're running a group. It's a business like any other, besides the Bang-Bang were, let's face it, freaks so they were more unstable than most. Only to be expected. So we did everyone a favour trying to keep women away, specially a girl like Laura, known dynamite.

J.J.L.: I have studied Laura's report on her side of the matter. She begins very openly, and gives a full account of conversations held, what everyone said, so on. Then—

N.S.: Yeah, well you know some people just can't keep their mouths shut. We could have managed everything fine—

J.J.L.: I was saying, Laura begins frankly, then suddenly there's a point she sort of closes down. Suddenly there's a funny sentence, like 'Following this conversation, I proceeded to the studio to see the damage.' Something of the sort. Conveys the impression she suddenly went impersonal and doesn't wish to commit herself to what really went on.

N.S.: Why should she? You've got to stick together, people will lie themselves blind. Look, I've got no kicks against Laura Ashworth—

J.J.L.: Excuse me but you do sound prejudiced.

N.S.: I'm not against anyone in this world. I've managed football teams in my time, live and let live I say. She was a good girl and nice-looking too, even if she did kind of stir things up. She kept them occupied, the Bang-Bang I mean. But the things she did, I'm no toffee-nose, right, but she wouldn't want to tell it, spell it all out, couldn't expect her to. We knew what was going on, but you wouldn't want me to say it either, not over TV, a family show, we all knew about it, I know the way things are. Everyone says they were musical geniuses, so what if they were kooky as well, let's leave it at that. It's all over now, isn't it?

J.J.L.: Then perhaps we might talk about the drugs aspect, and the Japanese stun gun.

N.S.: Okay, we had a violence problem. Barry was the dangerous one. Tom was quiet enough. You know what I mean. So we had to calm him down, Barry. The stun gun's harmless. There isn't a strait-jacket made that would fit Siamese twins, so we gave him sweet dreams instead.

J.J.L.: My understanding is that the stun gun is a development of the EEG, the electro-encephalograph, capable of switching the brain's activity from about ten cycles to one cycle per second, thus thrusting the victim into deep sleep. It's an illegal instrument in the West.

N.S.: About that . . . It never hurt him. See, if you injected Barry with something to lay him out, they'd both be out cold because their blood circulation circulated between them, see what I mean. We had to do something before he bust up the joint, what do you expect us to do? You know what Laura called me? An uncouth something. But I was the guy who got in close. Twice I had a black eye. He laid me out cold. He was possessed when he took off that Barry, real bonkers. He laid me out cold. She got some sort of a hold over them, okay, I let her borrow the gun occasionally – she put him out cold with it when it suited her purpose.

J.J.L.: An emotional hold over them?

N.S.: You know what I mean. Sex. That was all she was after. Put Barry out cold, have it off with Tom.

J.J.L.: And on the occasion when Barry regained consciousness while that was happening, there was presumably another row until she accommodated him as well?

N.S.: Look, I don't want to stir things up. Let sleeping dogs lie. Your guess is as good as mine.

J.J.L.: But you are making certain imputations against Laura Ashworth. It couldn't be, Nick, that this is prejudice speaking and that she was not guilty of such behaviour? There are rumours that in Dervish's day Laura was the victim of a mass-rape in which your name was involved. She hardly sounds the Lady Dracula type to me.

N.S.: Look, I don't want to . . . Look, who's stirring things . . . I said she was a sweet girl, din' I? What's past's past, that's my motto, and I s'pose that Paul Day's been shooting off his mouth again, Jesus. It doesn't matter now, does it? We're talking about history. It wasn't my job to stand outside their bedroom door like a bloody sentry, was it? I didn't want to know. I was their manager, not a wet nurse, don't forget.

J.J.L.: You had your orders from Zak?

N.S.: Zak was the boss. Same as Couling the lawyer said, our business is music, not morals. We aren't a bunch of kids who—

J.J.L.: Nevertheless, you feel defensive, understandably in view of what—

N.S.: You keep putting words into my head, things that were never there. I liked the boys and I liked Laura and I was only doing my job. I *made* them, I'm proud to say. Look, it's just we had a lot of crap all along, everyone exaggerating everything. It's all in the past, isn't it? You seem to forget we're talking about the greatest success story the world has ever known.

4

Zak Bedderwick's narrative

We built the Bang-Bang into a great success story. Inevitably, some of us sustained bruises on the way, but that does not take away from what we achieved. Scandal still circulates about the names of Laura Ashworth and the Howe twins – inevitably, since from the start the public insisted on regarding the twins as sexual objects. My intention here is briefly to try to show how what happened between the young people involved was natural and perhaps inevitable, and how it contributed to the art of the Bang-Bang. I am not a music critic in any sense. I shall just point out what is there to be read in the lyrics as they developed.

This may be the place to admit that I may have been a little unfair to Laura Ashworth in the past. We have to be wary of permanent or semi-permanent female hangers-on because of their possible disruptive influence on our groups. But Laura was more victim than vamp or vampire, of that I am now convinced. In ways which I shall indicate, she served as vital catalyst in the success of the Bang-Bang. (I must add that because of an unstable home background she was somewhat unstable herself and some of her public utterances should be disregarded. For instance, the Bedderwick Walker organization did not dismiss her; she simply ran away from an emotional situation she could not resolve, following the Scandinavian tour.)

The other vital element in that emotional equation was Paul Day, our songwriter. He and Laura were deeply involved with each other. As can be seen from the lyrics.

Day was an undersized youth who grew up in a Northern town and was drumming with various groups by the age of fifteen. By the time he joined Gibraltar as drummer/guitarist, he had had songs published. He became chief songwriter for the Bang-Bang, and played guitar with them.

On and off-stage Day presented great contrasts. Off-stage, it was difficult to get a word out of him; he would slink by without speaking if he could. Get him on the platform and a different persona took over. He then became a great extrovert personality; his inspired performances were highly regarded. To my personal regret, he has since left our organization and gone solo. The last I heard of him, he was working in the southern United States.

To my mind, Day's silences reflected an interior dilemma. He came from a broken home and had been wounded in the process. This led him to regard the Howe twins with sympathy from the start. Whereas they suffered from ostracism by the other members of the group.

I would like to clear Nick Sidney's name. He's a nice man and I could not do without him. But the Bang-Bang were very difficult and it was hardly surprising that they got him down at times.

The twins grew friendly with Paul Day. A strong bond formed between them. Day's songs reflect increasingly the way in which their tormented inner feelings awoke a response in his own mind.

It was noticeable that Day resorted to sci-fi imagery to express the division he and the Howe twins experienced between themselves and 'ordinary' life. A fairly early song, 'Year By Year the Evil Gains', appropriates the title of an actual SF story:[2]

[2] 'Year By Year the Evil Gains' in *New Writings in SF 27*, edited by Kenneth Bulmer, 1976.

> *City against city, town against town,*
> *Song against silences,*
> *My body against my brains*
> *As the entropic suns sail down –*
> *Year by year the evil gains.*

Later, sci-fi imagery helps express an attractive sense of distance, as in the immediately popular 'How's the Weather in Your World', which has now become something of a standard:

> *Our heads are together on the pillow –*
> *How's the weather in your world?*

The same year yielded 'In the Midst of Life', where the same sense of a tranquil alienation is conveyed:

> *And when you turn to me*
> *Silence falls into a green darkness*
> *And the light devours*
> *Cities, skies, your eyes.*

Less successful was 'On Tomorrow's Avenues', where the lyricism again conveys alienation, and the too-determinedly surrealist 'The Thunder of Daffodils Underfoot'. There is also 'Anyone's World', where the use of the unexpected number 'four' points to some actual experience; had the subject matter of the lyrics been stolen out of psychoanalytic textbooks, as one critic unkindly suggested,[3] we should expect the number to be two or three or even seven:

> *In anyone's world*   *Four is the most*
> *Time's under glass*   *People are mirrors*

[3] Colwyn Thomas, 'The Two Shots that were Heard Round the World', *Sunday Times*, 23 May 1982.

The idea that we can at best hope to experience no more than four people or character types, however numerous our acquaintances, is interesting. But it may be that the lyric is talking more directly of a small world containing only Tom, Barry, Paul Day, and – who was the fourth member? No doubt the fourth member was Laura Ashworth. The ambiguity in this song may not be deliberate, but Day was soon employing such devices with intent. Even the driving song, 'Valley of the Chateau', conceals a pun (The Valley of the Shadow of Death) made the more sinister by its being unstated – though pointed to by the rhyme-scheme.

> *Valley of the Chateau*
> *Valley of the Chateau*
> *Valley of the Sacred Chateau –*
> *Where none of us can take a breath*

The mood of the earlier songs is generally that of a child's fairy story. Where there is a menace, the central character is immune to it through his innocence. 'Two-Way Romeo' is an obvious exception to this rule, but that song was commissioned and written before Day had met the Howe twins. It is only a concoction. The recipe was mine.

We see Day being drawn gradually into a unique relationship with the twins and the girl, and learning to face it through his lyrics. He finds it threatening, as in 'Valley of the Chateau', and 'Probability A'. Sometimes its grotesquery can be expressed as comedy, as in the 'Serenade from a Cerise Satellite', with its repeated line

> *One girl   three loves   fifteen arms*

With the rocketing success of the Bang-Bang, the sexual imagery of their songs became much more open, for instance in 'Year of the Quiet Lips':

> *smiling without speaking*
> *perfect giving perfect taking*

> *healing, feeling, sealing, mutely appealing*
> *haven for all comers stealing*
> *quiet sips my summer year is here*
> *year of the quiet lips*

Patently, it is no dumb girl being addressed. The driving vigour that marked Day's performance on-stage becomes linked in the lyrics with a new outspokenness. Although the title 'Girl Outside the City' suggests isolation, both words and music speak of confidence:

> *The girl outside the city*
> *Let it all flow by*
> *Let it all flow by*
> *She's a part of me*
> *The typhoon's eye*
> *The typhoon's eye*
> *The air in the airport*
> *As we up and leave the city*
> *For the places where the pulse beats stronger*
> *Where the loving's madder where the nights are longer*
> *Where she's so much gladder*
> *Let it all flow by*
> *Let it all flow by*

Even in the period of the true love-songs, a note of reproach often sounds. Or it does on paper. What Day wrote tenderly, was belted out with contradictory ferocity. The performance gives us their version of the complex love affair.

> *Oh you are all things to me*
> *Lover and vampire*
> *You keep three lovers happy*
> *A phoenix of their fire*

48

In this world I'm love's tourist
Another head is dreaming of your beauty
Our love is a forest

(from 'Our Love is a Forest')

The line repeated in each verse, 'You keep three lovers happy', may seem like praise the first time; in repetition, it becomes more of a reproach. Even the freer moral code of our time has done nothing to extinguish jealousy.

The phraseology of the songs becomes more complex, the ideas move away from the traditional enclosed world of calf-love. No doubt it was Laura, with her more educated background and extensive reading, who influenced Day's vocabulary and the terms in which he celebrated her. This is most noticeable in the later songs, and in particular in the best song he ever wrote, his one song which mentions Laura by name, 'I was Never Deaf or Blind to her Music' (see Appendix), with such lovely lines as 'Time was, her alchemy was all upon me'.

This magical song, which one critic referred to as 'The Rhapsody in Blue of the Eighties', was included in the Bang-Bang's best record, 'Big Lover'. Here the Bang-Bang set aside what many regard as their natural coarseness, particularly in the three sci-fi tracks which are also included in the Appendix to this volume, 'Big Lover', 'Star-Time', and 'Bacterial Action'. These are by no means love songs. But they show Day rejoicing in the new perspectives which Laura brought to his life, and the new power of expression he found for them.

After this peak, there seems to be a recession. The structure of the love affair was probably too unstable to last for long. 'The Vocabulary of Touch' has certain ingenuity, but the musical form reaches back to the conventions of the thirties for its closing lines:

Wetness and heat and a tired kiss
All verbs expended

49

> *Your breasts   your shoulders   your eyelids closing*
> *The sentence ended*

Trouble developed on the Scandinavian tour. The Bang-Bang came to blows with Paul Day on stage. And as soon as they arrived back in England, Laura disappeared. My belief is that her Church of England upbringing had instilled strong feelings of guilt in her and she could endure the *ménage à quatre* no longer.

On that unhappy tour, the Bang-Bang performed live, for the first and last time, 'Passport to Another Planet', which I regard as Paul Day's farewell to Laura. A tired nostalgia is aimed at and achieved, despite ugly idiom in the first verse; in the last verse, isolation is again closing in on the singer.

> *You in your torn peace sleeping*
> *Come from a southern town*
> *Let me wake you with a cup of coffee*
> *Parting's going to bring us down*
>
> *Now with your passport to another planet*
> *You take your sex and sunlight away*
> *Life's going to be mere imitation*
> *Plastic lovers   cardboard day*
>
> *You dress that burning body*
> *And for the last time cling*
>
> *Already there's a glass case closing over*
> *The days when we had everything*

There was a glass cage closing over the age of the Bang-Bang. They were a phenomenon that came and went in under three years. The Howe twins were finished with the disappearance of Laura. Barry had some kind of emotional breakdown which I am convinced was nothing to do with overuse of the stun gun. I engaged a special nurse to look after them at Humbleden, as well as persuading their elder sister, Roberta Howe, to be with them for some weeks. Paul Day patched up his quarrel with them and then announced to me that he was leaving to strike out on his own in the States.

The Bang-Bang's three-year contract with Bedderwick Walker expired; neither side sought to renew. It is always better to be a coward and live to fight another day. The life of novelty groups is always limited. The twins returned to Norfolk and the obscurity from which they came. When all the charges of exploitation are made, I remain convinced that I was their benefactor. And the public heard a lot of good pop music.

Which is what I'm in business for.

5

Continuation by Roberta Howe

These accounts have covered the period of my brothers' lives during which they were world-famous. Much remains to be said concerning the later period of their obscurity. I am the one person with enough knowledge to fill in those missing months.

It was terrible dealing with them at Humbleden. When I arrived, poor Barry was exhausted enough to be bedridden, much to the frustration of Tom, who found himself tethered in one spot. I calmed him as best I could. He cried again, as he had many times, for a surgeon to set him free from his brother, although he knew that there was no operation which could spare the lives of both him and his brother.

'Then set me free and let me live! I'm the normal one!' cried Tom.

I soothed them as I so often had before. Paul Day, the guitarist, a nice quiet boy, spent a lot of time with them, mostly playing cards.

The day after Tom's outburst, Barry had a similar fit of anger, calling his brother a murderer and betrayer and I know not what else besides. They had a terrible fight, each trying to tear apart from the other, and falling off the bed in their struggles. Paul called for Nick Sidney, who applied his gun to Barry's head. It was the first time I had seen this done, but at least it brought peace.

'You'd better take us back home, Rob,' Tom said. 'We're all finished up as far as any cooperation goes. All I want's to be quiet and peaceful by the sea.'

When Barry came to, he seemed almost in a stupor. He said nothing. He staggered over to their wash-basin and Tom neither helped nor hindered, like he was pretending he wasn't there. I looked on Barry washing himself as of old, when he and Tom were children, and I noticed how he still took care to wash the silent face beside his. Whereas he would never touch any part of his brother's body. (That I know, and state it here to settle certain rumours that have circulated; other lies I will also settle in due course.)

Next day, we left Humbleden. Funnily enough, when Nick and the others came out on the steps to wave us goodbye, both Tom and Barry wept. I went with them back to L'Estrange Head. I had pleaded with father to let us move to somewhere less deserted. He refused. The time now arrived for me to feel glad that he had done so, hoping that wild nature, with the proximity of open land and sea, would have a healing influence on my brothers. Unfortunately, that was not to be the case.

I was pleased that Paul Day accompanied us on the journey home. He proved Tom and Barry's best friend, after all that had happened to them and all they had done, yet he scarcely said a dozen words all journey. To think they were world-famous yet so isolated!

Paul would not come over to the Head with us, offering as an excuse that he had to be back in Humbleden that night. I drove him to the railway station at Deepdale Norton. I got out of the car with him while my brothers remained silent inside. Paul said goodbye to them quite formally, shaking both their hands.

Nobody was about. The station might have been closed. Before he turned to buy his ticket for the train, Paul spoke to me quite urgently, in a low voice.

He said, 'I hope they'll be up to scratch soon. Something marvellous has died . . . I don't know . . . I want to tell you that your brothers and me had a good friend in Laura. I won't make no bones about it, she was a lover to all of us, a real prize girl and absolutely unorthodox how she carried on. That's why they were all against her, Nick and all . . .

'What she did was fine, really fine, nobody knows, though there are bastards about who tried all the time to finish it all. She's the best girl you could ever meet, a real life-giver, though she's gone now, more's the bloody pity. Oh, I'd have whitewashed the sky for her, believe me. Don't listen to any malice, we were the ones involved and we could tell you different if we was the kind to speak up, like those others.'

'I see. Paul, is there any chance I can get in touch with Laura if my brothers want to see her again?'

He looked down at the concrete steps and shuffled his feet.

'You ought to get her over if you can.'

'Have you any idea where she might be now?'

'She must be suffering, wherever she is. I only hope she can hold up. She always walked on a precipice. It was Chris Dervish, now dead, who did for her. He freaked her out on acid – maybe you've heard. Poor love, she tore all her clothes off of her. That lawyer guy Couling was down at Humbleden that weekend, and there was a gang-bang, with him involved and of course bloody Dervish, and most of the rest of the lads. Me too, yes, me too. She was so plastered. She was round the bend for a while after. I will say that I've never forgiven myself, and this time I have had my chance to make it up to her.'

'Did Mr Bedderwick get to know about this?'

'Couling went bananas after, paid us all to keep our traps shut. I really love Laura, Robbie, and would do anything for her, anything. It's not just guilt. She has a heart of gold, I mean I wrote all my best songs about her and that's about all I'm good for. I doubt if I shall ever write another song. I'm washed up. Maybe I can get myself together in the States.'

'Why did you all break up like this?'

He stared bitterly across the marshes.

'They was all against us. You can't imagine what the pressure's like. Success is a bastard. In the end she couldn't stand it. And Barry is cruel, full of rage against what he is. You know, it's his make-up, I don't *blame* him in any way.'

'Barry's never cruel. It's just what he's suffered.'

Paul scratched his head and did not contradict. 'Oh, he loved her same road as Tom and me did. You had to love Laura . . . Well . . . Anyhow, I thought I'd tell you so as you can understand. Hope you don't mind the grisly details.'

'Where can I get in touch with Laura?'

He gave me a light kiss on the cheek.

'If I knew that, d'you think I'd be hanging round here?'

A man came out of the station and pointed at a board we had not noticed. A sign on it announced that there would be no more trains that day. There was a one-day strike involving the footplate men of the region.

Paul would not come back to the Head with us. In the end, we left him standing in the sunshine. It was the last we saw of him.

That year was the very hot summer. The drought became so severe that wildlife began dying. All the windows of our house were open for weeks on end. Our poor old retriever Hope got a stroke from the heat and died; we buried him in the dunes. My brothers used to swim in the sea and the dykes every day. They took to going naked again, as when they were boys, despite my father's complaints, for we had many visitors to the bird sanctuary as summer advanced. The curse of silence had fallen on them.

A day came when Laura Ashworth showed up. She came over in Bert Stebbings' tourist boat from the Staithe just as if she was a tourist. First thing I knew, there was this woman tapping at the kitchen door. It was still funny not having Hope to bark at visitors. I dried my hands and went to see who it was.

She looked ever so old and smart at first, so I couldn't grasp who she might be. I'd expected a teenager, I don't know why, instead of this lady in her thirties, in a skirt and everything. I must have appeared a proper fool in my fluster.

She wore a tasselled suede jacket with a white blouse under, and a suede skirt and sandals to match the jacket. Her hair was brown and blonde in streaks, and her face also brown and slender, with pleasing light hazel eyes. She was willowy, with a nice breast and legs

55

– very attractive, I would say, once you got used to the shock. She was what I would call a lady, and self-possessed, as ladies are.

So I gave her a cup of tea and told her that Tom and Barry were away over the marsh somewhere. I asked where she had been since she disappeared but there was no straight answer to that. All she said was that she had changed her lifestyle but that she wanted to see Tom and Barry again.

To that I gave her no straight answer, but kept my trap shut. She tried some general conversation, remarking how bleak and flat L'Estrange Head was.

'Not when you get to know it, Miss Ashworth. There isn't a level space anywhere. We've got a lake and lots of little creeks, and in the more favoured spots elder and hawthorn grow – not to mention wild roses and blackberries. It's a very pretty place for them as likes it.'

She then asked me direct if I wished her to see Tom and Barry.

'Are you sure you should see them, Miss Ashworth? I ask for your sake as much as theirs.'

Did they want to see her? she asked. Did I think she would be bad for them? Not in any attacking way, more like genuine questions.

I went into some rigmarole about how she had left them once and perhaps things ought to stay that way. I wanted her to interrupt but she listened very patiently, sitting on one of our old kitchen chairs, holding her mug of tea, and staring out at the ruin of the abbey beyond our window. Suddenly I saw that she was silently weeping. I was glad my father was over at the warden's hut.

'I've no wish to be unkind, Miss Ashworth, but if everyone is going to get upset all over again, then perhaps it's better . . . I mean, did you consider enough before you came here?'

She dried her eyes and apologized. She drank her tea. 'You see, I've nowhere else to go. This bloody age we live in, we're all outcasts and strangers – it isn't just your brothers, Miss Howe. All the old values have disappeared, been laughed out of court, and we've got nothing in their place.'

'Still, that's not a very good reason for coming to L'Estrange Head.'

At that she laughed. 'Oh, I daresay the rot's set in here, too.'

So I poured her some more tea, and I said to her straight, 'Miss Ashworth, I don't see what you have to be upset about. If you loved my brothers and they loved you, then life was better for them than ever it was before. And we know such things don't last, alas. If you feel bad about letting them both make love to you at the same time, you don't need to do so. I don't see that's a disgrace. Forgive me for speaking frankly with you.

'I told them years ago that if they ever had a girl it would have to be that way, they'd have to share. Else it would be unbearable for the one who was left out, isn't that so? I'm pleased that such a girl came along.'

'Good God!' she said. She stared at me, then reached out and clutched my hand. 'I'm so used to opposition that approval takes me aback . . .'

'Well, I do approve, if it's any of my business, and I don't think you have any need to complain. Many a girl would think it was the peak of delight to have two good young chaps at the same time.'

Well, then she sort of laughed, and we both laughed, and she looked at me askance. She said she'd go along the beach and see how Tom and Barry were.

At the back door, she paused and said, 'I suppose you think I'm here for more of the same thing?'

I smiled at her. You could not help it. 'Probably,' I said.

An odd thing about our Head was that everyone remarked on how flat it was; yet it was not at all. There were endless places to hide, as Bert Stebbings and I could tell you. So I didn't see Laura or my brothers again until the long dusk had fallen, when they appeared at the back door, staggering, both with lips and noses bleeding. No sign of Laura.

'You've been fighting again, you bloody fools,' cries my father, jumping up and flinging down his encyclopaedia. 'One of these days, you'll kill yourselves.'

'I'm putting up with him no longer,' cries Barry, making over to the draining-board, and seizing up the kitchen knife. Tom resists him, trying to trip him over. Both swear violently while they wrestle.

Barry makes as if to cut the two of them apart through the living flesh. They have nothing on, and sand falls from their sweating bodies as they abrade each other in the struggle. My father and I both jump up. I scream. My father, being powerful, finally manages to get the knife away from them. They both fall back against the sink, never able to get away from each other, the flesh that joins them stretched into bars.

When they have calmed down slightly, I ask where Laura is. It almost starts another fight.

Tom is in a kind of cold fury, his face very pale. 'I can say or do nothing with this madman at my throat,' says he. 'It is not possible to talk to her or touch her without his interference.'

'He tries to monopolize her,' cries Barry. 'So what do you expect? She's gone off on Bert's last boat to the mainland. I wish I were dead, I wish I were dead. Even more I wish this parasitic bastard were dead.'

The tendons and skin between them were contorted as they held themselves as far apart as possible, Barry knocking his head against his sleeping one in his longing to tear himself away from his brother.

'Is she coming back?' I asked.

'Why should she?' cried Tom. 'Why should she, to be pestered and threatened by this bully.' He burst into angry tears. Always infuriated by such displays, my father shouted to him to stop.

As for me, I was greatly disappointed. I had hoped Laura would stay and help the boys be more normal. She would have been company for me. A feeling of desolation came over me, and I ordered them both up to bed.

Watching them fight their way upstairs, reflecting on their perpetual enmity and my father's general indifference, I wished that when they had left they had never come back. I wished Bert would marry me and take me away. I stood paralysed in the middle of the room, wishing myself a thousand miles off.

My father put the knife down, settled himself at the table and scanned the bird encyclopaedia again.

'It's botulism, that's what it is, Robbie,' he said, 'that's what's doing for the mallard.' He stroked the dead duck that lay by his hand.

'I wish it would do for all of us!' I rushed out and ran away over the dunes.

After Laura's visit, the last stage of my brothers' struggle began. When I returned to the house and crept up to my bed, I could hear them arguing and shouting in their room. The noise got so furious at one stage that I went out and paused before their door. Of course my father slept through it all, dreaming peacefully of the mallard dying in the summer marshes, no doubt.

My brothers were having a vulgar old row, details of which I had best not repeat. Tom wanted them to go off and find Laura. Barry said he was being greedy and refused to leave the Head; they could rape women visitors who came to see the birds. They brought in other charges against each other, unresolved quarrels from the past. They had fuel enough.

I was about to creep back to my room when they started another fight. In no time Barry was shouting, 'Come on, come on, I'll break your back for you, you gutless little git!' I heard the window swung wide, and a scuffle. I ran in – just in time to see the strange double-backed creature leap from the window.

Running to look out, I saw them pick themselves up from where they were sprawling. Punching, kicking, biting shoulders and jaws, they struggled away into the dark.

I called. They paid no heed. I returned to my bed.

Next day, that deadly antagonism was continued. They appeared mid-morning, fighting to eat and stop the other eating. They broke a chair and struck each other with bits of it. For the first time, I could not find it in my heart to be patient. They ran out, a mad animal fighting itself to death. After that, they did not intrude in the house again. They had become feral.

The heat wave continued, in perfect days and brazen nights. I swam last thing in Compton Water, when the visitors had left, relishing the calm last light in the western sky. Ducks continued to die, and not only ducks. My father doggedly piled up poisoned gulls, Canada geese, mute swans, snipe. Our little lagoons and ditches were sick, our lake choked; their waters had turned the colour of gherkins, thickened by algae. Dead fish, bream and the like, floated to the surface. Foul smells spread across the Head.

During the nights, I would wake, hearing my brothers scream and swear outside, sometimes near, sometimes far away. During the days, when the heat rose, I would occasionally see them running with that gait personal to them, across the dunes, in an endurance race of their own devising. I hardened my heart against them.

A conservation officer from the National Naturalists' Trust came and examined our dying wildlife. The drought had properly upset the balance of nature. A strain of bacteria causing botulism had bred in decaying ooze in the exposed beds of ponds and ditches drying under the sun. Their poison was attacking the birds' nervous systems. Every day, deaths mounted. My father dug trenches among the dunes and buried the victims, grebes, gulls and ducks.

The heat, the atmosphere of death, and the disappearance of my brothers brought a suspension to life. Everything waited.

The only punctuation to our days was the arrival of two men from the NNT to help us save some of the affected wildlife. Father and I worked with the men, day after day, pulling a hand-trailer across the undulating grass and marram. We worked all the way to Great Aster, the marsh terminating the Head to the east. We visited Norton Lake, our one stretch of fresh water, which was replenished through dykes and wooden sluices from Deepdale Marsh, inland. The eight-acre lake looked beautiful, with purple loosestrife in bloom along its banks. But it was sick. Dead fish floated belly up. When we stirred the bed of the lake, it gave off a reek of hydrogen sulphide. We collected two black-headed gulls, a great-crested grebe, and a cormorant too ill to dive and escape us. Botulism Type C had attacked all these birds. The cormorant's neck was so weak that it could not lift its head. Some of these poor creatures would recover when moved to uncontaminated water elsewhere.

Sometimes, I looked up from our task and spied my brothers

some way away. They were watching us. The whole landscape shimmered in the heat – it was difficult to believe they were there. As we worked along the southern fringes of our little domain, along by Little Ramsey, Great Ramsey and the saltings, towards Overy Mussel Strand and Great Aster, I would look inland and see a silver thread of holiday traffic winding along the coast road. I realized how isolated we were.

Father hardly spoke from dawn to sunset. His heart was breaking to see his creatures die. Yet some creatures flourished in the drought. We saw grass snakes for the first time on the Head. Sand lizards scuttled everywhere – pretty little nervous creatures. Most unpleasant was a plague of ladybirds, which sprawled copulating in their millions all over the house, getting into beds and food and clothes, piles of them everywhere like fresh blood.

The sun baked my unfortunate brothers black. They were starving each other, taxing each other to death, wearing each other down, regardless of consequences. I feared that they devoured carcasses of poisoned birds. Visitors to the sanctuary were terrified by them. A London journalist on a weekend trip to Blakeney filed a story with his paper which appeared under the headline 'Minotaur in a Mallard Sanctuary'. We had a special boatload of tourists after that. My father drove them off by firing his sporting rifle over their heads. He was almost as strange as his sons.

Our little isolated world stank of death. I hung bunches of sea lavender and the pungent sea wormwood in the kitchen. I locked the doors at night. My brothers cried outside my window – blessings, pleas, obscenities. I could not bear it. I went away in Bert Stebbings' boat and stayed with my aunt at the Staithe. But I had no place there, and returned to the Head late the next day.

Bert took me back in his boat. It was nine in the evening as we chugged up The Run. L'Estrange Head was deserted of its daytime visitors. Its bare extent lay quiet under the last of the sun. I could see the abbey ruin and our house against it, with a light burning in the kitchen, where my father would be reading or stuffing a dead bird. Never before had I felt the desolation as hostile.

My brothers heard the chug of the boat's engine as we rounded into Cockle Bight. They came running like a four-legged beast into the shallows towards us, brandishing sticks in their outer fists, shouting, cursing me and Bert.

'They've gone proper barmy, Robbie, my love, that they have – I wouldn't trust yourself to them,' Bert said. He shouted out to them to control themselves.

They paused. They stared out across the darkening waters towards us. The Deeping Sands light started its quick flashing out to sea. For the first time in my life, I was scared of my own brothers. They were not my brothers any more. Instead, they were something – elemental is perhaps the word.

'Come back home with me, Robbie,' Bert said. He stopped his engine.

Those were the words I wanted to hear him say. Tom tried to wade out towards our boat. At once Barry lifted up his right inner arm, and locked it behind Tom's head so as to thrust it forward. Of all the indignities they had inflicted on each other, this move was one, I felt sure, they had never managed before, because of the tightness of the ligaments binding them together.

Tom kicked out at Barry's legs and a fight started. They fell into the swelling sea, bellowing. They disappeared, though terrible thrashings marked where they were.

'Oh, quick, Bert!'

Without a word, Bert let in the clutch and we surged forward. He made a sweep round, cut the engine, threw out his little anchor, and jumped overboard, all in one practised series of movements. I jumped in after him. The water was up to the top of my thighs.

Bert got on top of my brothers and started pulling. Tom's head came up, water pouring from it, his mouth a wide hole gasping for air. Barry's head came up, and the third head. But Tom grabbed it by its hair and dragged them under again. Bert caught him round the throat and wrenched him above the surface.

Somehow we dragged them to the nearest bit of beach between us and dropped them there. Tom was still fighting and coughing and swearing but Barry was too exhausted even to do that. We worked at his lungs, but he merely groaned. He was unconscious, his face livid. Suddenly it was dark and chill.

Glaring up at me with an alarmed expression, Bert said, 'He looks real bad. We'd best take them to Dr Collins' clinic in Norton.'

As he spoke, Barry groaned louder and went into convulsions, sitting up – still unconscious but his eyes staring – and bellowing for breath. His face was distorted, his neck thick. He flung Tom about in his agony.

'Quick, it's his heart!' cried Tom, clutching at his own heart.

Bert and I stood up. The sky was darkening overhead with night winding in across the marshes. Barry's noise was terrible – both his and that other face were black as they writhed in pain.

'It's a coronary attack,' I said. 'Oh, Bert! Better not to move them. I'll go and get Dad. You go back in the boat and get Dr Collins. Quick as you can. Tell Aunt. Look, ask Aunt to phone Henry Couling, that lawyer, will you? She has his number. We may need his help.'

'Don't leave us!' Tom cried.

I was suddenly all cold and practical. Without waiting to see Bert go off, I told Tom to lie as still as he could and went on the run across the dunes for father.

The rest of that night is best not told in detail. When Barry's attack was over, father and I got him with Tom's help back to the house. We tucked them up under blankets on the floor of the living room. It was best not to attempt the stairs. Barry was in a deep slumber, seemingly more dead than alive. Both his face and the other one were flushed. Tom also complained of pains, which was scarcely surprising, considering their connecting circulatory system. His breathing was fast and shallow; he was sweating a good deal and looking thoroughly frightened. When I bathed his head and shoulders, a crust of dirt came away.

Bert came with Dr Collins on the low tide at six the next morning, when colour had newly returned to the world about us. It was impossible to make headway up The Run in a small boat against an incoming tide.

Everyone loved Dr Collins, mainly because she looked like sixteen years of age and had the stamina of a carthorse. She was a small neat woman with bobbed hair. She examined both of my brothers before giving them an injection which put them out. Her diagnosis was that Barry had suffered a thrombosis. It was imperative to get them to the hospital in Holt quickly.

Nobody argued with Dr Collins.

Father roused himself from his self-absorption for once and took charge of things. We shipped Tom and Barry over to the Staithe in Bert's boat, and Dr Collins phoned for an ambulance. Before the ambulance arrived at the Staithe, Barry had another violent attack. Both the boys were in a bad way. The terrible heat did not help matters.

On the way to the hospital, Barry had a further seizure, and died.

6

Statement by Dr Alyson Collins

Roberta Howe has asked me to write a note about the Howe twins, and of course I am happy to do so. The Howe twins are as celebrated in the literature of teratology as are the Siamese twins. However, I intend this to be a personal record, not a medical paper.

The sibling hatred that existed between Tom and Barry was accentuated by their inseparability. In character they were totally different, both dominated by an impaired parent-relationship. This encouraged neurotic passivity in the case of Tom. Under ordinary circumstances, Tom would have signified submission in any rivalry situation by withdrawal; linked to his aggressive brother, he was unable to withdraw, and so was in a perpetual anxiety state, his self-assertive faculties constantly over-taxed. Which is not to imply that he was not often the aggressor; as psychotherapists understand, worms turn, and Tom in hysteria frequently attacked his dominant brother.

In most reminiscences of the Howe twins, Barry is generally cast as the villain. I am less certain of this. Admittedly he was aggressive, yet it is doubtful if he would have attracted attention had he been free to pursue his own course. There is some evidence of obsessional neurosis in his attempts to control Tom, but this is hardly to be wondered at, when we reflect how he was forever unable to act as a free agent capable of spontaneous action.

Anxiety quotients were high in both Tom and Barry. In childhood and after, they had been examined by experts at irregular intervals. After every examination, they suffered traumatic outbursts of activity, characterized by violence. This suggests masked fears about the severance – a traumatic event following which they would have to make their way through life alone, as individuals, unsupported in a world which had already graphically demonstrated the inadequacy of parental love.

Their meteoric rise to being pop superstars reinforced the underlying fears that either would have been useless on his own; while their sexual jealousy rendered continued propinquity intolerable. Resultant tensions destroyed them.

My understanding is that constant high anxiety quotients promoted serum cholesterol levels in the bloodstream which promoted serum cholesterol levels in the bloodstream that accelerated a narrowing of the arteries of the heart. The formation of blood clots was promoted, and so the coronary attacks occurred. Since the Howe twins had a communal circulatory system, it is a matter of accident that it was Barry rather than his twin who suffered from the thrombosis.

We were fortunate that Sir Allardyce Stevens, whose work on artificial hearts and pacemakers is well known, happened to be at Holt Hospital when the twins arrived. Sir Allardyce was attending a symposium, and had had occasion to examine the twins professionally during the period of their success as the Bang-Bang. He immediately took charge of the case.

At this juncture, Barry Howe was already dead. Which is to say, his heart pump had failed and was merely fibrillating in response to the linked pump of Tom's heart. Tom had responded to the shocks to his system with hysterical attacks. The male nurse with him in the ambulance, Mr V. S. Porter, had administered a sedative, and Tom was still unconscious when the double body was wheeled into Holt operating theatre.

Sir Allardyce's examination showed severe infarction of the right ventricle, with necrosis of cellular tissue there and in the adjoining superior vena cava. The layman must understand that this examination entailed open-heart surgery in which cardiac catheterization was employed. In other words, the preliminary steps towards a heart transplant were already taken before Sir Allardyce decided that a heart transplant was necessary. I explain this because criticism of that decision has circulated, mainly thanks to an ill-informed lay press. The decision represented a small step on, and an inevitable one if the Howe twins were to survive. No competent surgeon in Sir Allardyce's position would have decided otherwise.

An APPCOR (Auto-Powered Prosthetic Cardiac Organ Replacement) of the correct specification was to hand. It was installed in place of the defective organ, and the installation proceeded without a hitch.

I was moved by my first sight of the Howe twins. They were both handsome young men. It was an ill turn of fate that they had not entirely separated in the womb. Given this conjoined condition, they should not have been encouraged to survive post-natally. Such is my professional opinion. I am aware of certain moral considerations. I am also aware that medical men have a natural streak of curiosity; given all the wonderful modern adjuncts of their profession they are sometimes tempted to prolong life in order to see what will happen, without, regard to the grief incurred by the survivors. In this respect they are little better than Victor Frankenstein, bringing a creature to life without any thought of what might follow.

Now Sir Allardyce was patching one such example of regardlessness with another of the same kind. He was a brilliant surgeon who had a brilliant opportunity come his way; it was hardly to be expected that he would not take it.

I travelled with the twins in the ambulance from Deeping Staithe to Holt, and was present during the 'death' of Barry. My own panel, my own patients, awaited me back in Deepdale Norton. I returned there as soon as possible, since I was unable to make myself useful at the hospital. However, such was my interest in the case that I drove back to Holt when evening surgery was over. Sister Carrisbroke showed me to the ICU – and there were the Howe twins, with Tom propped up on a pillow and taking soup.

Barry lay back beside him against the banked mattress. His eyes were closed. His complexion was pale and blotched in comparison with the healthier colour of Tom's face. The other head lay silently against Barry's, in its usual position. Barry's breathing was normal. Tom was cheerful. As so often in APPCOR cases, the recovery rate is impressive. When I drove back again to Norton, I gave Roberta Howe a lift from the hospital. She spent the night at her aunt's in Deepdale Staithe. She was tired but cheerful.

'I never seen Tom look so relaxed and content,' she said.

It was not for me to spoil her happiness by reminding her that the everlasting sibling struggle would resume as soon as Barry regained consciousness. At her Aunt's, a message awaited her from Mr Couling, the lawyer of the show business agency which had employed the Howe twins as singers, saying that financial support would be forthcoming from the agency. So I left Roberta in a state of subdued relief.

For the next few days, the media were full of accounts of the APPCOR operation, and photographs of the Bang-Bang were in circulation again. Then Sister Carrisbroke phoned me while I was taking evening surgery. She had alarming news. Barry had not recovered consciousness. Barry remained dead, despite his new heart.

On several occasions, the expanding frontiers of medicine have caused us to alter our conceptions of dying. Ever since the sixties of this century, it has become increasingly difficult to define the critical point at which life can be said to slip irretrievably into death. The Jacobean poet was near to the truth when he said that 'Death hath ten thousand several doors for men to take their exits'.

After surgery, I got in my car and drove the nineteen miles to Holt. Doctors rarely think about death; on that journey, I had to force myself not to.

Sister Carrisbroke's professional manner was reassuring.

Brain cells undergo rapid amortization once their supply of oxygen is cut off. Thirty minutes after oxygenation ceases, irreversible deterioration commences. For some hours following Barry's thrombosis at Cockle Bight, Tom's heart had had to bear a double load for both bodies to survive. In terms of actual work, it had to pump one hundred and sixty gallons of blood an hour, and to keep that heavy fluid moving through the equivalent of 120,000 miles of veins, arteries and capillaries. It failed to provide circulation enough for Barry's brain – to be precise, the vital neocortex, the essentially human sectors of the cerebral hemispheres.

Barry lived physically because of the APPCOR. Psychically, Barry was dead.

The APPCOR functioned perfectly. It would not restore the defunct brain tissue in the middle skull of those three tormented Howe skulls. Tom was now coupled to an animated corpse.

'And the . . . third head?' I asked the Sister.

She looked askance at me. 'The EEG shows a speeding-up of cortical and sub-cortical activity of low voltage in the third head.'

'What does that imply? It's waking up?'

She said, 'Barry's head is electrically dead. The third head appears to be moving towards a working state.'

'My God, what does Sir Allardyce say to that?'

'He's back in London, but keeping in touch.'

'I should damned well hope he is. Tom?'

'Since Tom knows nothing about *that*, he is pretty happy.' She laughed with an edgy note. 'He thinks he's got the place to himself. He's won his battle to be alone.'

Three weeks later, the twins, only one of whom was alive according to classical definition, were permitted to leave hospital. Their devoted sister, Roberta, met them at Holt and took them back across The Run to L'Estrange Head.

The last act of the affair was played out there, and we have only Roberta's record of what occurred.

7

Conclusion by Roberta Howe

It was hard to think of them as just Tom. After all, Barry was still *there*, his body working perfectly, thanks to the machine heart, the APPCOR. There was a difference, though, and in the main a difference we all enjoyed. Barry did not fight any more. He was meek and submissive – or his body was, I should say. This was such paradise for Tom that he was content to sit all day, in the house out of the heat, and generally in his bedroom, where he could stare across the ruins to the sea.

Dr Collins came over in Bert's boat to see how we were getting on. There was nothing to report but calm. Barry was gone – I can't say dead, because that never made sense to me, with his body walking round, whatever was technically correct. His head now lolled forward and his neck was lax, like the birds attacked by Botulism Type C. It often lay peacefully against the third head. To strangers, Tom and his double-body would have presented a strange sight.

Pleased though I was to have peace, the situation worried me – that I will not deny. The day after they were back on the Head, I went over to the Staithe to see Aunt Hetty and shop. Owing to the tourist trade, Mr Bowes at the stores had many more goods than in the winter, when there were only us locals to cater for. He had a rack of paperback books going cheap, among which I spied one entitled 'The Brain Simply Explained'. I bought it and took it back home to read.

Simply explained or not, much of the book I could not understand. One passage, however, stuck in my mind.

An arterial system delivers the oxygen to 10,000 million neurons. Similar intricate systems go to compose the enormous complexity of the brain. Small wonder if occasionally a connection malfunctions, as in a television set. It co-ordinates and regulates the muscular systems of the body, preserves a lifetime of human experience, and functions as the centre of human awareness. The paradox is that there are still sectors of the brain whose function we do not understand and, consequently, there may be types of awareness of which we are still unaware.

That was in Chapter One. 'Small wonder if occasionally a connection malfunctions'! That must have been what happened to poor Barry. Something had gone wrong in their bodies at birth – it was reasonable to assume something had gone wrong in their brains.

I thought about the strange happenings that occur in our brains, and wondered how the whole business could have come about, while father and I worked the foreshore during that long afternoon, looking for sick birds. And that night Tom had the first of his three dreams.

Well, I put it like that. Later, I recollected that during the previous night – the first night he was back with us from the hospital – Tom had cried out in the small hours; I had heard his cry, then fallen back to sleep.

This time, it was about three o'clock when he began to scream. It was a choking noise which gradually became louder. I had never heard anything like it before. I was out of my bed and running to him almost before I had come to my senses. I darted past my father's room and into Tom's.

It was stifling hot in his room. The window was open, but there was not a stir of breeze. The September moon was two days off full, and its light poured in. Outside, beyond the dunes, glittered the sea. As I ran to the bed I saw that Barry's arm was across Tom's throat. It was withdrawn as I entered, slithering quickly under the sheet.

I soothed Tom's forehead and comforted him until he roused properly. He broke into long deep sobs which convulsed his body. I sat there, muttering words of love to him, feeling so glad to be of some little help. All this while, Barry's face lay close on the pillow. It was that of a man sound asleep – expressionless but hardly what I would dare call dead, whatever the medicos said.

As Tom calmed down, I noticed that the eyes of the other head were slightly open. There was a glitter as of liquid under the heavy lids. Venturing greatly, I reached out and put my right hand over the eyeballs. I felt a distinct tremor beneath my fingertips.

At that I took fright. Giving a yell, I ran out of the room, back to my own. Standing by my bed, trembling, I heard Tom call me.

I went to the door, peering into the dark of the landing.

'Tom? You all right?'

'Please come and see me, Robbie. I had an awful dream.'

Of course, I mastered my courage and returned to him. He had propped himself up a bit, and the other two heads lay against each other like two bowls, half-hidden by sheet.

I held his hand. We just sat and looked at each other in the cool moonlight. His face glittered with sweat.

A curious impression settled on my mind: that this was my dream, that I was still in my bed. Both the noises and the silence, the light and the dark, seemed to me in that instant – I believe it was just an instant – to be more like something that goes on in a sleeping head than in reality.

Then Tom said, 'I've got to tell you my dream,' and the impression dispersed.

I suggested that we went down and had a cup of tea in the kitchen. As he pulled on his jeans, I saw that the Barry body was already wearing its pair; Tom had not bothered to undress it. The double body came down the stairs after me. Switching on the reading lamp downstairs, I looked fearfully at the third head, but it gave no sign of intelligence.

While we drank our mugs of tea, Tom related his dream, with a few comments here and there from me.

'They gave me sedatives every night in hospital . . . Tonight was different. Open the back door and let some breeze in, Robbie! There's nobody out there to harm us . . .

'Well, my dream. It was so macabre, so connected. Not like a real ordinary dream . . .

'I was in a forest and rain was falling. A heavy, slow rain. It must have been falling for a long while. The forest floor was flooded. A steady stream pulled against my feet, making progress difficult.

'I could not see my way ahead. As I staggered onward, I kept buffeting myself against the trunks of the trees. They grew so close that my shoulders were bruised with repeated knocks. The journey had been so long. All the branches of the trees, high above my head, had intertwined. Darkness ruled in the forest. And yet – you know how these paradoxes occur in dreams – everything seemed bright, as if lit by an inward light.

'By another paradox which seemed natural at the time, I was not myself but a horse, or some other four-footed animal. I'm not sure what. Perhaps a donkey – a pack-animal – because I was loaded down and consequently clumsy. And I was trying to get away from someone I hated. That urgency propelled me through the loathsome forest. The someone I wanted to get away from was helping me escape. He rode upon my back in a great raised saddle, draped with rugs and strings of jewels. With a black whip, he lashed me on.

'Blood burst from me. It fell like rubies, each large gobbet solid, gleaming, clattering to the ground. Yes, clattering to the ground, to dry stony ground.

'Where that ground was in relation to the rest of me, I can't tell, for I seemed to be still in the flood, and my difficulties increasing. When I glanced down, I saw that the flood-water had receded, leaving a carpet of thick mud. I saw that I was planting my hooves in the open mouths of great toads. No matter how I tried to avoid them, my hooves plunged into their open mouths, nailing them by their throats to the ground.

'My distress was so great that I began to cry in my sleep. I rolled, yet I could not roll over, for now another great lumbering beast was beside me. It was more like a giant sort of maggot or mummy – something corpse-like. Despite that, it was as if we were both galloping forward at a great pace. I could not out-distance the mummy. It was being ridden by a chimpanzee.

'Describing it like this, the dream sounds like a silly collection of wonders. It was all one situation – immediately understood, going on for ever. Suppose there is a life after death – if we were called on to describe our lives, we might be forced back on similar recital. I mean, we might not be able to describe it except as a list of its events. Like a fisherman who sees a river just in terms of its fish. Yet my dream was about the river – it wasn't about any of the events I've described at all, but about something else entirely. No. I'm telling it wrong.'

Tom gulped down some tea, then started again.

'I was aware that, whatever I was doing, I was actually doing something else. Oh, I know it sounds confused, but sometimes in dreams a state of confusion comes over as marvellous clarity.'

'Perhaps you were only half asleep,' I suggested.

'Perhaps we are never more than half awake . . . Anyhow, it now seemed as if I was no longer the horse, and had never been one. I was being carried on the back of one. It was a beautiful milk-white mare, and its rocking movement through the forest was sweet to me. But I still had to carry the great swaddled maggot with me. The trees were still flashing by, and it was dangerous to remain among them. Their trunks, I saw, were carved with elaborate carvings.

'Now the trees became more widely spaced. I gained courage. As we broke free of them altogether, I raised up the great maggot, lifted it above my head, and cast it away.

'Until the very second of parting with it, I had no interest in its nature. As I threw it, I became overwhelmingly curious as to what it was. Have you ever had the experience of being with a friend and finding nothing whatsoever to say to him; and then, as soon as he was gone, you think of a dozen important things you wanted to say? I met an old man when we were on tour in the North who told me he had married a girl he was madly in love with. Their marriage went all wrong right from the start. He hated her, he wanted to kill her because she disappointed all his hopes and broke his heart, and they got divorced. And immediately, he said, immediately he was free again, all the hate fell away, and he just longed for the girl, loved her more even than before, and could never look at another girl.

'A similar abrupt change of feeling came over me as I threw the maggot, or whatever it was, away from me. The bundle opened as it fell and I saw a small child's – a baby's – face looking up at me, rosy-cheeked, smiling, and absolutely innocent of any expectation of disaster. Then it hit the mud and at once sank into it, still smiling and trusting. To the last moment when its face was sucked under, it smiled up at me uncloudedly.

'Again there was division of feeling. Part of me rode on, haughty and glad to be free. Another part was overcome by grief. Great sobs rose up in me and cascaded from my mouth and nose and eyes. They fell in the form of diamonds, which rained to the ground and clattered there as previously my blood had done. My own noise woke me.'

He sat there for a while, head between his hands, so that three bowed heads confronted me.

'It was as if all that was good and valuable in my body was going from me,' he said. I clutched his hand, and we sat there in silence. Slowly the ashen light of dawn seeped in.

When Bert brought the first lot of tourists and birdwatchers to Cockle Bight, I was there waiting for him. He ferried me over to the mainland, where I borrowed his bike and cycled over to Dr Collins' surgery in Deepdale Norton.

She took me through into her office and made us both a cup of coffee as I poured out my tale of woe. I even brought myself to tell how the third head had opened its eyes.

'You mustn't be frightened,' she said. 'It's nothing – supernatural.' But she flicked her gaze away from mine, as if she was also alarmed.

'If Barry really is dead, if it's just the APPCOR that keeps his body – well, from putrefying . . . then couldn't your surgeon do the operation and cut Tom free?' I asked. In the silence, I added, 'I know it would be a major operation.'

'I'm sure the possibility has occurred to Sir Allardyce,' Dr Collins said. 'Look, I'll phone him. I've got the number of his rooms in Harley Street; sit down, Robbie.'

Sir Allardyce was away. He was expected to look in to collect messages at 12.30. Then he was off to attend a one-day conference in Milan. His secretary promised that he would phone back at 12.30.

So I killed time. I went to see my Aunt Hetty, I had a drink and a sandwich in the pub with Bert and, at 12.20, I was back at the surgery. The call came through at 12.50.

Sir Allardyce had already been giving the matter consideration and was in consultation with his colleagues. I was to be reassured that the matter was still very much on his mind.

This much I heard, watching Sir Allardyce's talking head on the vision plate, before I interrupted. I told him that it was urgent, and that Tom was heading towards a breakdown, dragging a corpse round with him, and that I feared evil things unless help for him was forthcoming.

'I know exactly how you must feel, Miss Howe,' he said. 'But this is an absolutely unique case, and we must proceed with due care. We discharged your brother from hospital because he was unhappy there, but in my opinion it would be best if we brought him into a London hospital for observation.'

That sounded sensible to me. I said I would accompany Tom wherever he went.

Sir Allardyce looked at a calendar I could not see. 'Today is Wednesday. I shall be back in England on Friday. I will have my secretary arrange to have your brother collected in an ambulance on Friday and brought direct to London. Will that suit you? We will ring back and settle all the details of the arrangements with Dr Collins.'

So it was left. Only two more nights, then Tom would be in proper hands. I returned to the Head with relief.

Tom was restless that afternoon. He went out and wandered in the direction of the lake, returning not long before sunset. After exchanging a word with me, he slipped upstairs and played his guitar for half an hour. 'Two-Way Romeo' was one of the numbers. Then silence.

I cooked him some sausages and chips and he went to bed early. Father was stuffing a dead tern. I went out for a walk in the moonlight, strolling along what we always called The Feather, a fine curve of sand sculptured by wind, with water on either side of it. The night seemed limitless. I longed – oh, I don't know for what!

Father had retired when I returned. I crept softly upstairs, pausing outside Tom's room. Silence. I went to bed and slept eventually.

When I woke, I found myself sitting up. Clouds had blown over the moon and it was dark. Outside was the endless sound of the sea; inside, the noise of father snoring. Nothing else.

Getting up, I padded barefoot down the passage. Something compelled me to enter Tom's room.

The dimness fluctuated as clouds moved away from the moon's face. I saw three heads lying on the pillow. All were still. I approached. Tom's eyes were closed. Barry's eyes were closed. The eyes in the other head opened. Slowly, it turned towards me. The eyes opened wider.

As if this muscular exertion was a severe strain, the mouth fell open. Never to my knowledge had it opened before. I wondered if it contained teeth, but in the dull light only a black cavity could be seen. The eyes glittered. The general effect was one of imbecility. We stared at each other.

The noise of my own heart thudding made me move. Slowly, never letting my eyes leave the glittering ones, I edged towards Tom's side of the bed. The other head moved, keeping me always in sight. My outstretched hand reached Tom's shoulder, and I shook him, calling his name softly.

He muttered and stirred, but I could not rouse him. I shouted louder. Now a noise came from the black open mouth – a kind of a laugh, grating, dry.

'Tom!' I yelled. I slapped his face. He had a mug by his bed, half full of water. I dashed it in his face. At last he sat up.

'It's all sand,' he said.

'Oh, Tom, what's happening?' I cradled his head in my arms, and at last he was himself again.

'The other head's alive, Tom, it's coming alive.' We looked at it, but the eyes were closed again, the neck limp, in its usual position.

'I was dreaming about it.'

'What's its name, Tom, what's its name?'

'It hasn't got a name,' he said impatiently. 'It's dead, same as Barry.'

He climbed out of bed. Again I saw how perfectly coordinated were the movements of the other body, which Tom now controlled. But I felt something monstrous about him.

He went downstairs. There was nothing for it but to follow. He was splashing his face under the tap.

'Tom? Let's go and have a swim.'

'I was dreaming that I heard music. Perhaps it was your voice far off. It was a totally different kind of dream from yesterday's. It was more coherent – much more like a movie in some ways. But it was very malicious.

'And it went on for a long while.

'I dreamed I was a sort of tame creature or perhaps a person on a beautiful island – a small island much like an unspoilt England, with thickets and glades and lovely little intimate dells to be in. The only other people on the island were my master, who was some kind of alchemist – he wore rich gowns and a crown, which sounds silly but it was splendid in the dream – and his daughter, who was about my age and whom I loved dearly. She had long golden hair and a laughing mouth, and I remember seeing her dance by the edge of the waves. I dived in and out of the waves like a dog.

'All sorts of things happened, magical things, and they were all fun. I was tremendously happy. I could do magical acts as well, charm birds out of trees, whistle fish out of water, fly with the golden-haired girl over hills and the thatched roofs of villages, capture the sunrise.

'One day, I found a secret valley with a waterfall at the far end. It seemed to me the most delightful place, and I flung myself into the water. I think she was there too, and we were climbing up and up the cascade, laughing, when the alchemist caught me.

'He was furiously angry. Nothing I said made any difference to his fury. He had me trapped and I was dragged, as if by wolves, to a dark part of the island. I had never been there before. I realized that I was not a grand person. Seeing myself through the eyes of the alchemist, I realized that I was just a kind of rough animal, a sport. All the time that I was being dragged over broken ground, I was trying to shout and explain that I really was what I thought I was, not what he thought I was.

'The terror wasn't from the journey so much as from this conflict of viewpoints. Because, in the dream, I could understand his conception of me to some extent, yet he could not understand mine, although mine was the truer one. Mine went deeper. Mine saw me from inside. Yet his view triumphed, simply because he was stronger – remorselessly strong.

'He took me to a great leafless tree. It must have been an oak. I saw its branches spread all over the sky like cracks in heaven. It was freshly split down the middle, so that its insides were open and all pale and yellow and glistening, like a disembowelled rabbit. Splinters hung all round the split, like the jaws of an animal with ferocious teeth. It opened still wider when the alchemist spoke. His voice was like thunder. I was crying for mercy.'

Tom paused and wiped his face.

'Telling you all this, I see it begin to sound like a dream about fear of punishment after sexual intercourse. But it wasn't half as simple as that in the actual dream. Because this wizard owned me, and there was a sort of counterpoint in the dream about how in fact he was quite powerless or rather he could invent nothing good, which was why I was malformed; whereas I had invented all the delights of the island. It's difficult to explain in words. When he grabbed me, he rolled up all the good things as well, just as if they were the pattern on a Persian carpet. Carpet and I, we were thrown into the gaping entrails of the oak. Whereupon the alchemist slammed the tree shut and locked it with a great golden key.

'Immediately, it was like I had been transmuted into another person. I was just walking down a road in a rather boring way. I wasn't on the island any more. I had the carpet and I had the girl. She walked with me, much diminished. She had been writing a diary but now had hidden it and would not even tell me where it was; I did not wish to know where it was, but her silly refusal to speak about it chafed my spirit – I wanted free communion between us.

'Because of this, I led the way into a small village in a snug river valley, where we were surrounded by singing people all having great fun. Somehow I despised them. I was apart from them, though I sang with them. Yes, and I can even remember the song I sang . . .

'No, I have forgotten the tune, but I remember what the song was about. It was about a planet entirely covered by water. Over the ages the water became conscious. It flew away to another solar system, leaving a great world of sand where the tide had gone out for ever. I ran laughing over the golden sand, tremendously happy because again I was free. Things were hatching out of the dark damp sand, growing, spinning. They evolved into enormous complex castles and people and – oh, unimaginable shapes. It was wonderful.

'These inventions of my song invaded the snug river valley. Nobody paid any attention to them. Everyone left me. There was just the sand. Someone was standing by me, explaining. I did not like what he was saying, particularly as I could not see him.

'"Now you understand how the ocean became intelligent and developed life," he was saying, going into some long obscure scientific explanation.

'As he was speaking, I saw he was referring to a head which was growing out of the sand. It was more or less like a human head, but at the same time I could see inside it. It was all divided into different sandy floors and rooms, rather in the manner of a complex dolls' house. From it were pouring sandy thoughts. The thoughts were so powerful that I felt that they were overcoming me, and soon – I cannot tell you what terror I still experience when I say it – *the whole universe was becoming nothing but dry sand thoughts*. I saw that the stars shining overhead were just gobbets of sand.

'I was full of disgust. Even the sunlight was composed of fine particles of sand which threatened to suffocate me. With an effort, I began running for safety. The sand-grains stung my cheek. Even running was painful. Behind me, the head was growing bigger and bigger; it was virtually a planet in its own right.

'Looking down, I saw my limbs, my body, were composed of sand too. They began to crack and break . . . I scarcely dared wake up in case the dream proved to be real.'

We sat unmoving. At last I asked Tom if he would like a swim, just to convince himself that he was perfectly well.

'Just let me be. I'll sit here a while and recover. You go to bed, Rob.'

I pointed at the other head.

'That thing was awake, Tom. It is alive, it has thoughts. I don't think it is any friend of mine or yours. Suppose it wakes up fully and you're reduced to unconsciousness . . .'

Tom stood up. I saw anger on his face. 'You get up to bed, girl, and don't talk nonsense. Leave me alone. I've been meddled with all my life.'

'But what do you think, Tom? Aren't you afraid? Why not talk about it?'

'There's nothing to talk about. Leave me alone.'

His manner had changed so abruptly that I was scared. I made my way reluctantly upstairs. My father was still snoring securely; it would have taken the Last Trump to wake him.

Well, I thought, one more night to go before we get Tom to proper care.

In the morning, he was gone. Father wanted me to do various odd jobs, and it was afternoon before I could strike out across the

Head and find him. He was sitting dejectedly under the shade of an elder tree.

He seemed to be his old self again, saying he was sorry for his angry outburst. I coaxed him back home and gave him something to eat.

As the day wore on, he was increasingly listless. I kept looking at him when he was looking away. Barry's head was sunk down useless on to his chest. His cheeks looked gaunt and withered. The other head – was it not tense, as if feigning sleep? Hadn't its face filled out? Wasn't its hair less grey, less dead-looking?

Nameless fears filled me; I thought, if only we can get through the night, tomorrow the ambulance, London, proper care . . . I had not dared tell Tom yet what was planned. In a good mood, he would do as I bid. And he would surely want to be a separate person on his own if that was possible.

Towards dusk, I persuaded him to come and swim with me. Father sat at his table, watching us go, smiling vaguely.

The visitors had left. One or two solitary lights dotted the distance. The sea was flat, its surface heaving as if in a stupor. Not a wave broke. A leaden mist moved slowly over the sea like oil, the token of another day's heat already in preparation.

I stripped off my clothes and flung myself in the water. Tom waded in. As he launched himself, the other heads came up, and Barry's limbs went through swimming motions just as if he were alive. Just their two outer arms moved, the way of swimming they had adopted long ago. We did not stay in the water for long.

Above us in the sky shone the full moon, the Norfolk harvest moon.

'I think I'll sleep better tonight,' Tom said. 'I wish Laura was here.'

So we went to our bedrooms. Despite all my anxieties, I was soon fast asleep.

No sooner had my eyes closed – so it seemed – than the screaming started. It sounded like the snarling of a pair of wild dogs fighting. I staggered up, full of sleep, and again made my way to Tom's room, like a somnambulist. Again I had a strong impression that I was dreaming. Everything was precise in detail yet faint over-all, like a dream.

I went down the corridor like a swimmer, very slowly. When I entered Tom's room, the snarling had stopped. He was propped up in bed, smiling at me. He had arranged the sheet over the other heads.

It was so light in the room with the moonlight that his teeth gleamed when he yawned.

'What's happened? What was all that noise.'

'I had another dream.' That was all he said. He yawned again.

Tom, are you all right?'

'It wasn't anything at first. I can't remember ever having the same feeling in a dream, or in real life. I was just nothing. Surrounded by nothing, I can't describe it. I had been sucked dry of all life, although I wasn't dead.' There he paused. When I thought he was going to say nothing more, he began again, in a dull voice.

'There just seemed to be wind about, blowing hither and yon. What slowly appeared was like part of my thoughts, at least at first. I was surrounded by desert. Only gradually did I realize that there were soldiers marching through it, whole ranks of them. Only they weren't soldiers; they were knights in armour. They trailed on through the sand with automatic tread.

'As I followed them, the revelation came that they were robots, things of metal, without consciousness. They were governed by a great distant machine, a vast metallic bowl like a flat face, like a huge radio telescope, which stood on the distant horizon.

'We marched and marched. There was a typical dream contradiction, because the lifeless robots occasionally fell and died and decayed as they hit the sand, so that we found ourselves marching over skeletons.

'Another contradiction – though it was all negative, nothing, it also seemed vastly important.

'The desert sloped down towards sunset and night. All the robots were marching into night, going from sun to dark and disappearing. It looked frightening. I didn't want to go that way. As I tried to leave them and go another way, I discovered that I had been turned into

84

a robot too. I had no control over myself. I was forced to march into that destructive cloak of night.

'The night was artificially generated by the distant machine. I knew something about that machine but was unable to remember what. Now I was entering the dark, crying in despair.

'A powerfully built man stood at the entrance, flogging everyone in.'

Tom paused, yawning again. Frightening though his dream sounded, he was telling it in mild tones, as if he were bored. I stood at the foot of the bed, listening, not moving.

'My emotion was so strong that there was a sort of break in the dream, almost as though I was being given time to dissolve. I felt that I was sinking to the bottom of an ocean – or rather, to the bottom of a multi-layered city which was drowned in an ocean. I could see lights, and people laughing and talking inside open windows as I floated down.

'As that awful downward drifting continued, I got to know more about the people. There were myriads of them, myriads and myriads, and they were all working on one immense project. The project was secret and involved building a super-weapon which would obliterate life on Earth – or wherever I was. The scheme went forward under immense secrecy, which was why the city had been built at the bottom of the ocean.

'Learning this information filled me with a sense of doom. I know the whole dream is filled with doom, but it was sharpened by the obsessive secrecy with which everyone worked. They were doing such a diversity of things towards the one end – pickling vegetables and embroidering cloth as well as working on all kinds of machines; apparently everything that was done in the city contributed to the one hideous end.

'What made it worse was that everyone was enjoying themselves in a quiet way, despite the oppressive conditions and the secrecy. As I passed along the submerged street many a person I saw giving a crafty laugh or a sly snigger.

'It began to seem funny to me, too, although I knew it would all end in a mighty explosion . . .'

Again Tom paused. He snuggled down comfortably against his pillow. I waited for him to continue, but time lengthened and he said no more.

'Tom?'

He was asleep again. His breathing was even and regular.

I felt as unreal as a ghost, standing there at the foot of the bed. Drawn by an unknown compulsion, I moved round to where Barry's body lay covered. Grasping the corner of the sheet, I moved it: then, with an effort, pulled it down.

Barry's head lolled uselessly. But the other . . . Its eyes were regarding me. They glittered from under heavy lids, like oil. The mouth was partly open.

I brought myself to speak. 'Who are you?'

No reply. But it moved, craning up on its neck to regard me better. I took a pace back and repeated my question.

Then words formed in its mouth. 'You are part of my dream . . .'

The voice was suffocated, as if it came from under a pile of mouldy pillows.

'You aren't Barry. Who are you?'

Again a long wait, during which we stared at each other. Then it said 'My name is . . .' The word it spoke was instantly lost. I could not remember it as it was spoken and have been unable to since. 'I have been penned in this tree all my days.'

'You are not in a tree. You must be dreaming. Go back to sleep.'

The sense of effort when it spoke. 'Now I am escaping from the entrails of the tree. The two wicked ones who imprisoned me will be punished . . .'

Then silence. Then, with little regard for what it had just said, 'One has already died, one remains.'

On me was the strong spell of a dream from which I was unable to break free. 'You're wrong, you're wrong,' I was repeating, but it took no notice.

'I'll wake Tom,' I said.

Immediately, it was in action. Barry's body leaped up at me. Its arm came out and I was seized viciously by the wrist. The move was totally unexpected. It pulled me down to it, getting its other hand behind my neck.

I saw myself about to be dragged down on it, to have my face in contact with that face. At last I managed to scream. What a joy to make that noise, as when I first gave cry!

Tom's eyes opened.

He was immediately aware of what had happened. He twisted his body and struck the other's arm. The other released me and tried to grasp Tom by the throat. In its anger, it looked much like Barry, whose head lolled peacefully between the struggling pair.

A fearful battle took place between the two of them. I rolled off the bed and ran in fright to waken father. I burst into his room and beat him on the shoulder. Swearing, he came to his senses at last and climbed out of bed, grasping his sporting rifle which stood propped against the chair by his bedside. I had heard a rumpus on the stairs. When we got out there, the pair were down below. Father rushed down in the dark, shouting, I followed. Sounds of crashing and the back door bursting open.

The table in the living-room had been overturned. Father and I ran to the open door. It was almost as light as day outside. The twin figures were distant, still struggling together but making away across the low dunes. Father raised his rifle to fire, but I seized it and dragged it down, screaming at him.

'Are you mad, are you dreaming? That's your son out there!'

'They should never have been born.'

He stood where he was, wiping his mouth over and over again with the back of his hand. The struggling figures disappeared into the night.

Switching on the light, I looked at our old clock ticking on the mantelpiece. I saw with horror that it was only just a quarter to one in the morning. I wanted Bert to help me, and Dr Collins – anyone – but there was nothing we could do till daybreak.

Sleep overcame me. I dozed off in the old chair. When I woke, dawn was moving in across the flat prospects outside. I was stiff and cold.

The table was still overturned, the door still hanging open. There was no sound in the house. I boiled up the kettle and made myself a mug of tea. No one would be stirring in the Staithe yet. Soon I would switch on our flashing emergency light outside, our way of calling the mainland. Aunt Hetty would see it when she rose at six-thirty and would go to summon Bert.

I padded outside and looked about. The early mist had not yet dispersed. The low line of the mainland, with its woods and church towers, was obliterated. We might have been on an island out to sea. Nothing moved. I tried calling Tom, but there was no answer.

Somehow, I did not feel like venturing too far from the house, but I took a stout stick and walked towards The Feather. There I strolled with my feet in the wavelets, as common and lesser terns started up all round me. The tide was at its full. A boat was chugging up the channel.

The sound of that engine, the lines of the boat, and that figure in the blue jumper standing at the tiller, were all dearly familiar. It was Bert in his boat, amazingly, gratifyingly early.

A moment later I saw he had a passenger. Not Dr Collins. Too early for her. It was Laura Ashworth.

I ran across to Cockle Bight, calling to them.

Soon Bert was helping her ashore. I caught his look of admiration as he gave her a hand. She was wearing the same clothes as last time I had seen her, a brown suede outfit. She gave me a big hug.

'What are you doing here?'

'I saw about the heart transplant on someone's television. I was in Spain, in the south. I got here as soon as I could.'

'Laura came up on the milk train from London,' said Bert admiringly.

'And got you out of bed, I see,' I said. But there were more important things to talk about. 'There's trouble, Bert. I know Tom's in fearful trouble.'

As quickly as I could, I told them both what had happened.

'I'll stay and help you find Tom,' Bert said. He tied up his boat and we headed back to the house.

'This new creature who's taken possession of Barry's body,' I said. 'It seems to think that all its life so far has been stolen from it. Now it wants to take over Tom's body as well. They are caught in some terrible battle I don't understand.'

'Another psychic battle! Poor Tom's been involved in a psychic battle all his life,' said Laura.

'It could be over today.' I told them about the hospital arrangements.

Laura had not slept all night. I made her some tea, and then we set out to search the Head. She and I set off together eastwards along the seaward side, Bert took the landward side.

We had the sun in our eyes. We said little to each other. Every now and again, we called Tom. I pictured him struggling with that new nameless thing, the evil face close against his, his feeling of absolute desperation. I longed to be with him. I longed for Laura to be with him.

After about two hours, we heard a distant shout. We answered it. We stood where we were. Bert appeared over a distant dune, waving once. Immediately, I knew something was wrong. Laura and I looked into each other's faces and set off in Bert's direction.

His face was grim. As we came together, he took my hands without looking at Laura.

'Tom's over by the observation post, my love. Don't go.'

'I must go to him.'

'He's dead, love. Laura, you look after Robbie, will you? I'm going to get back to the boat fast as I can, and I'll come back with the police.'

He gave me a kiss and was off across the uneven ground at a jogtrot.

'I got to go to Tom,' I said.

She came with me.

The joined bodies lay on the landward side of the observation post. A bank of cobbles was piled against one side of the wooden hut and they lay together on the cobbles. All the way, I had been unable to believe Tom could be dead. Directly I saw him, I knew. The two joined bodies were huddled in positions the living never use.

Laura gave a cry and took a step ahead of me. She too stopped. You could go no nearer.

On the brow of the other head was a black and bloody contusion, where Tom had struck it with a stone. Tom's head was almost locked with Barry's.

His right hand still clutched a big scallop shell. After knocking the other out, he had performed an operation of his own. The other's naked chest had been cut to pieces by the scallop. Beside the frightful wound lay Barry's artificial heart. Tom had ripped it out of place after laying the chest open.

He must have died almost as soon as the other. The load on his heart would have been great. Now his frenzy was past. The lines of his face were relaxed. From his twisted position, one eye looked up into the morning sky.

Laura squatted down in front of him and began to weep.

These painful events have now receded into the past. How vividly I recall crouching by that mutilated double body, my knees painful on the cobbles, crying, and hearing the flies buzz.

Finally, Laura and I gathered ourselves up and went back along the strand. I summoned father. Later, Bert returned with a police officer. Bert took me and Laura away from the Head. The bodies followed later in another boat.

I never knowingly failed my two brothers. Perhaps I failed the other. Perhaps I could have helped him too.

Although I sometimes dream of him, those dreams have now shed their terror. His lost life – what did he think, experience . . . ? Was his a dream or a life? I don't know what to make of it, any more than I know what to make of anyone's life, come to that.

The days are full enough, now that I have children of my own. They too are making their journey through the forests of life. Sometimes when they are in bed, Bert and I play the old Bang-Bang

LPs to ourselves. Then I look out of the window and across the waters, to where father still lives out his solitary life on L'Estrange Head. Everything vanishes in time, like the music when the record stops playing.

R.S.

Appendix

Big Lover

Go to my lover and say
    That Earth is nothing but a star,
It's just the merest light-point
    To even its nearest neighbours.

Serenade her with the facts
    Concerning life on Earth,
Its startling brevity of tenure
    Give her cosmology and music

To show her she is my lens
    Through which I view the universe,
My eye, my sun/My big lover
    My galactic one.

Love is a Forest

The animal and the sublime
    Make you so versatile,

You keep three lovers happy
    Yet torture them meanwhile.

In this world I'm love's tourist
    And take a package tour of solitude
Our love is a forest.

Oh you are all things to me
    Victim and vampire,
You keep three lovers happy
    A phoenix of their fire.

In this world I'm love's tourist
    Another head is dreaming of your beauty
Our love is a forest.

Your loveliness is legend,
    A statue I would carve,
You keep three lovers happy
    And satisfied to starve.

In this world I'm love's tourist
    Our love is a forest.

Bacterial Action

Although the world fills up with men
    Their numbers do not match
The numbers of the swarming swarms
    Of creatures living in our skin.
They have their nations and domains,
    Pleasant jungles, deserts, streams.
They live, beget, and leave no trace
    For eye to see or mind to judge.

They've no Byzantium or Rome,
    Yet they were there, in smock and gown;
Proud Caesar was their planet too,
    In time their old prolific line
Will speed commensally with us
    And all unknowing win the stars –
Yes, ultimately win the stars
           Unknowing

Star-Time

We – who had survived the journey
To the forty-seventh millennium
Where dark starlight grows on bushes
And eyes house laughing kookaburra birds –
We sat drinking *xwaszha* in a café
With boys and beauties whose grandfathers
Were in their cots when we set out.
It was triumph
It was triumph
My happiness took me to loving hearts and couches
Yet we who had survived the journey
Knew that all the while our memory
Stayed with those elegant grey seas
Curling over what was Europe.

Just for a Moment

Just for a moment think about spun glass spinning
    Moving in a low December's sun,
Shining above rough dark secret meadows
    Lying where the leaf-choked marshes run.

Just for a moment think about a perfect colour
　　Fading on the margins of the sea,
Lapping against a pallid shingle pathway
　　Leading to a castle tall and free.

Just for a moment think about pure silence
　　Shining above a distant mountain peak,
Looking towards the radiant eye of moonlight
　　Falling upon the contours of your cheek.

Just for a moment visualize time absolute
　　Dwelling through a planet's unlived years,
Passing over far untravelled tundras
　　Turning where the long-haired comet steers.

Or just for a moment think about a moment
　　Let movement colour silence time all flow,
About your lovely waiting head unknowing –
　　And then you'll know my love's bounds,
　　　　Then you'll know.

I was Never Deaf or Blind to Her Music

No, I was never deaf or blind to your music, Laura

I breathed more oxygen in her company,
　　Reached higher speeds and a wider sort of skies
And dredged for her secret salts and alkalis.

　　It was just that the days closed in,
A new motorway went up between her place and mine.
We couldn't agree on the merits of Stockhausen
There were quarrels about my drinking habits
We stopped going to gigs together

And then there was that trouble with her employer
  Never properly explained
I started breeding wire-haired terriers
She said she lost her respect for me when
  I couldn't give up smoking.
But no, I was never impervious to her vistas
Plunging into the lake of what she was
She stormed me every day like valiant deeds
And my head was as full of her as poppy seeds.
It was just that the weather changed,
My job took me up Sheffield every week.
I felt a compulsion to join the scientologists
She got mad on Dresden china pieces
We became hooked on television
She suddenly wanted to see the Sierra Nevadas
  And dance the true Flamenco
With a bearded Dutchman studying zoology
When I think of her driving round Granada
  I long for our time again.

No, I was never deaf or blind to her music,
Time was, her alchemy was all upon me.
She packed every moment like a picnic box
She was air and sea to my hills and rocks.

I was never deaf or blind to your music, Laura.